I NEVER SAW PARIS

I Never Saw Paris

A Novel of the Afterlife

HARRY I. FREUND

CARROLL & GRAF PUBLISHERS
NEW YORK

I NEVER SAW PARIS
A Novel of the Afterlife

Carroll & Graf Publishers
An Imprint of Avalon Publishing Group, Inc.
245 West 17th Street, 11th Floor
New York, NY 10011

AVALON
publishing group incorporated

Library of Congress Cataloging-in-Publication Data is available.

ISBN-10: 0-7867-2054-9
ISBN-13: 978-0-78672-054-5

9 8 7 6 5 4 3 2 1

Printed in the United States of America
Distributed by Publishers Group West

Dedicated to the memory of my parents,
Miriam and Milton Freund

As a shepherd tallies his flock, and makes each sheep pass beneath his staff, so dost Thou record and number and take account of every living soul, setting a limit to every creature's life and passing sentence upon all of them.

—From the prayer of Rabbi Amnon of Mainz, 11th century

CONTENTS

Part I

-Shock-

1

Part II

-Lives-

19

Part III

-Angels-

131

Part IV

-Conclusion-

173

Part I

Shock

All right, so I listened to my wife. After all, I've been doing it for nearly forty years, I should have stopped now? Boy, is she going to feel guilty.

So there I was standing at the corner of Fifty-seventh Street and Park Avenue, minding my own business, waiting for the light to change. My mission was to buy blue shirts, Jane insisted that I buy more blue shirts, they bring out the color of my eyes, she said, they give me a little color. My luck, there was a sale at a fancy store on Fifty-seventh, go there, she said. So I was waiting at the corner, to my left a great-looking woman in her fifties, a real Manhattan type, all dolled up, loaded with jewelry, great body, great legs. To my right, a handsome young fellow wearing a sport shirt and the tightest jeans I ever saw; I noticed the lady glancing at him approvingly. Me, she didn't seem to notice. At sixty-four, I'm much more age-appropriate for her than he is but, hey, looking is free, let her look. And that was my last relaxed thought on earth because that's when I noticed the car coming straight at us, right onto the sidewalk. An old man was slumped down at the wheel, eyes closed. His was the last face I ever saw in my life.

And now look, an emergency crew is arriving, I can see everything down there on the corner. They're examining me and the others, we're lying there all askew, and for the first time now I see an old black lady on the ground behind me. I had heard her scream, what a shriek, but I hadn't seen her before. After some time, the crew pronounces us all dead. What a waste, those lousy shirts, I could have lived without them. And I had finally booked that trip to Paris for Jane's birthday; I never wanted to go but Jane did. Twice before we had planned on it and cancelled and now this. Three strikes and you're out. So I never saw Paris, never will; poor Jane will have to go alone, she'll have to go to Chanel without me.

She doesn't know about me yet, it takes time, they have to identify me first, then they have to reach her. And I never remembered to tell her about the new stock account I opened at Merrill Lynch, but that's all right, she'll get the monthly statement, she'll show it to Bobby, he'll figure it out. He's my boy, he doesn't miss a trick, he'll find it, over seven hundred thousand dollars in it, I don't know how I forgot to tell her.

God, I wanted to see the kid, Bobby's firstborn, due in three months. That's unfair, where's the justice in that? My first grandchild, I don't even know if it's a boy or a girl. Bobby knows but he wouldn't tell, he wanted to surprise us. If it's a boy, maybe they'll name him after me, although who knows what his wife will do. Maybe my name isn't fancy enough for her, nobody uses Irving anymore, I bet she won't do it. They'll use something with an *I*, maybe Ian or

Ivor, and I'll be lucky if they even do that. You know what, I'm dead, how insulted can I get, what's the big deal?

I'm really feeling very relaxed, considering what I've just been through. My mind seems clear, but my emotions feel constrained, a little distant. There's my blood on the street, there's that poor fancy lady sprawled next to me still clutching her big pink handbag, and that young guy, he tried hard to escape, I could hear him groaning, grunting with the effort. And that black lady, her gray hair disarranged. What a way to go, so mindless, so public, on the corner of Fifty-seventh and Park, people milling about, pointing, commenting. No decorum, no dignity. The police are arriving, they'll chase away the crowd, they'll cover us up, enough is enough.

It's strange, floating like this. I read a couple of times about people who died and were then revived, they felt they were floating, they usually saw a light, a tunnel of light. Well, I'm floating but I don't see any light yet. And I don't feel my body, my shoulder doesn't ache like it always does, and my knee isn't killing me. I've just been hit by a car and I feel no pain. So this is it, nothing, just my mind working, very little in the way of emotions, this is it? You live for sixty-four years, you go through plenty, and then that's it? Some old guy runs you over and the story is over. All the planning, the worrying, all the work and then Jane sends me for shirts and that's it. For blue shirts, I had to have blue ones, Jane insisted. The color blue killed me; if I looked better in white shirts I would have lived. I needed those damned blue shirts, thanks, Jane.

Now I'm seeing some light, beams of light. I think I'm moving up, the scene down below is further away, I'm definitely moving up. And I'm not alone, there are other faces moving toward me. That one is definitely the face of the old man behind the wheel, that's the last face I saw before the impact. And there are the women, and the poor kid, can't be more than twenty-nine, thirty, he looks scared. We seem to still have our bodies and yet mine feels ethereal, cloud-like, useless but nice, snug, safe. And now we're all hovering together, no distinct expressions perceptible on the faces that I can see, expressions benign. And a deep silence, deeper than any silence I can remember, a relaxing silence, peaceful. And now that light again, we are bathed in light.

Some time passes, that's okay with me. No sense of urgency, no appointments to worry about. Just silence and light. Not bad, maybe this is it, maybe this is eternity, suspended animation, silence.

Oh, no, come on. Cut it out. Come on, not an angel, looks like an old guy with wings, floating toward us, wrapped in a cloud-like sheet, looks like my mother's uncle Benny but with wings. This is a dream, it's got to be a dream. I'm going to wake up soon, I'll be in my bed , it will be five or six in the morning and I'll have to pee. Jane will be fast asleep next to me. I bet it was that corned beef I ate last night, who can digest that at my age? I'm dreaming. There can't be angels, angels are mythological figures, the pathetic imaginings of primitive man. I haven't believed in angels since I was eight or nine years old. Come on, wake up, enough already.

The supposed angel drifts into our midst. His wings brush against my face, soft, not feathery, just plush. He lingers among us, filling the space among the five of us, all aglow with light.

"Welcome," he says. "I am the angel Malakh. I am appointed to assist you in the transition between life and after-life and to answer any questions that you may have about the process. Please do not be overly anxious, this process is a gentle and illuminating one and the very fact that I have been assigned to you should be reassuring, as I am specifi-cally trained to deal only with normal souls. Those who are at the extreme ends of the moral spectrum are processed by specialized angels, also the souls that are insane, the unhinged ones, the nuts. I handle only the normals, so by definition you are on the right track already, you are where most souls end up. Because of the enormous soul load to which we are subject, I am also limited to deaths in Man-hattan and to people who are believers or claim to be believers, at least notionally, in a personal God. If you are not such a believer, that's perfectly all right, but I cannot handle your case and will pass you on to an appropriate angel. I would appreciate it if you will respond and affirm some basic facts. It is possible for you all to speak and I will call upon you each to do so. Let's begin with you, Mr. Caldman," as he turns to me.

"You are not dreaming, Mr. Irving Q. Caldman, sir. You have shed your earthly body, you are left with an illusory facsimile of it, and are now in transition. You will not awaken, you will not return to your previous existence. You are now present in the early form of afterlife. Please confirm that you are the soul that I believe you to be, the husband of Jane Rosen Caldman, father of Robert Z. Caldman, the president of Caldman and Company, an investment firm. You were an active board member of several philanthropic organizations, resident on Fifth Avenue in New York and on Horsebone Road in Bedford, New York. Religion: Jewish. Is this correct?"

I nod in the affirmative. For the first time I feel shaken emotionally, I feel a frisson of icy fear, almost a refreshing sensation, an echo of the emotions I am accustomed to experiencing. I really am dead, this is really happening to me; I am not waking up from this one.

The angel turns to the elegant lady. She has regained her pre-accident appearance, her blonde hair is carefully coiffed, she is wearing an expensive suit, heavy-duty jewelry, and she is again clutching a big pink alligator handbag. She must be

in her fifties, a knockout for her age. "You are Clarissa
Bowen, married twice, currently to Andrew Bowen, mother
of Twinky, profession: personal shopper. You reside on East
Eighty-fourth Street, Manhattan. You are a member of the
Junior League and are active in the Botanical Society. Reli-
gion: Presbyterian."

"Correct," the woman replies, her voice cultured and
dignified, her manner poised.

"Brett Taylor," continues the angel, "not married, never
married, profession: interior decorator, residing on East
Twentieth Street. Religion: Roman Catholic."

That's the boy, taller than me, a big, powerful kid. Looks
like a weight lifter, nice face, dark hair, a refined expression,
all-American type.

"Yes," says the fellow, "I'm a good Catholic. I just took
communion last Sunday."

"Excellent," says Malakh and turns to the black woman.
"Essie Mae Rowder, widow, mother of Charles and William
Rowder, grandmother of three, profession: domestic,
residing on Bergen Street, Brooklyn. Religion: Evangelical
Christian."

The lady nods, she seems calm, more relaxed than the
rest of us. She's quite old, her hair has turned gray but her
dark skin is smooth, almost unlined. Big, sweet brown eyes,
kind eyes, she's not smiling now but you can see the potential. A sunny disposition, a warm-hearted lady. She's dressed

in a nondescript way, practical, sensible. Malakh turns to the remaining soul, continues.

"You are Mendel Perlow, widower, father of Avery Perlow and grandfather of two boys. You own a candy store on Eighteenth Avenue in Bensonhurst, Brooklyn. You reside above the store. Religion: Jewish."

Mendel must be in his seventies, almost bald, a lined, weary face with intense dark brown eyes, steely eyes, a tough old man. He's wearing an old worn suit, no tie, a man who gives no thought to his appearance. The old man does not immediately respond. His gaze is steady, his expression dour as he stares at Malakh.

"Mr.Perlow?" Malakh prompts him.

Another minute or so passes in silence and then the old man speaks in a heavy European accent.

"So you're an angel, so if you're an angel then there is a God. Right? No angels without a God. So He exists, huh? I wouldn't have bet money on it. You forget to mention one little fact from my life, Mister Angel, you forget to mention that I was an Auschwitz boy, that I graduated from Auschwitz when I was seventeen. Such a fact should be mentioned, not left out. You should tell this God of yours, He has an Auschwitz boy on His hands here, maybe He'd be interested. Who knows?"

"Sir," Malakh replies, "I understand and, believe me, everything is known here, nothing is forgotten. Not the slightest injury or insult, let alone such suffering as yours. Please, be patient, just be patient."

"Patient," repeats Mendel, "I should be patient. This God of yours, He takes my life when I'm driving. I killed some innocent people with the car. This is justice? This is decent? That I should have been responsible for all these people dying? This is how a life should end, I didn't see enough death and destruction, I needed to die in such a way?"

Clarissa breaks in. "It wasn't your fault, sir," she says, "nobody is blaming you."

Essie Mae nods in agreement. "We're all in God's hands," she adds, "nothing happens that is against His will."

I remain silent. The man is old, frail, maybe he shouldn't have been driving at all. I should forgive him? Not so fast, he should have taken a taxi if he was not so well. Brett is also silent; he looks dazed, vague. I wonder how much of what's happening is being absorbed by him.

Malakh speaks up.

"Look," he says, " I've been on this job for a long time, I've seen it all. Believe me, Mendel, you're not the first survivor I've handled and not just from the Holocaust. I've had Armenians, Bosnians, Rwandans, you name it, I've had it. Please take your time, what's done is done, and no one is blaming you for anything. What good is complaining now? Each of you souls will have your chance to stand before the

High Court, each of you will have your shot. My job is to help you prepare. I'm only here to help. You know how much sorrow I've seen? You think it's easy? But I've got to do my job. We angels have an annual day of judgment, we're also judged. If we fail repeatedly, we face punishment; we can even be relegated to human status, demoted to human life, God forbid, to have to live in your world. Believe me, I take my work seriously. I'm here to help you."

Mendel closes his eyes and is silent. The rest of us are, too. Again a deep silence seems to descend upon us, it's comforting, it's peaceful. I rest in it and think to myself, so there is still emotion left in us, Mendel is angry, the ladies are forgiving, the kid is dazed, and me, I'm alert, I'm interested. So there really is a God, if there's a High Court then there is a Judge. If He is omniscient, nothing can be hidden, all the years I bummed around, the women, everything. This could be serious, if there's a God there could be punishment. Maybe severe punishment, this is no joke. And I'm the most likely one in this group to be in trouble. The old guy survived Auschwitz , he'll get off light. And that black lady, she probably never hurt a fly. Clarissa, the worst she ever did was probably spend too much at Bergdorf Goodman. That kid, silly name, Brett, what could he have done, he was a decorator, what did he do, mismatch some fabric? But me, in all those businesses, how many times I fired people. Remember that guy, what was his name, that idiot I hired with all those kids, he lived in New Jersey. He was some salesman, he couldn't find his asshole with both his hands, I had to fire him. He cried when I did it, tears fell down his cheeks. Listen, I gave him a big severance, I was generous, he had six kids, I think. What could I do, the guy was terrible. And Laura, remember her, I knew I was taking advantage of her, I was young and she was really great-looking. I was nice to her, I realized she was doing it to keep her job, but I was generous, when she left to get married we gave her a big sendoff, gifts. Look, I wasn't perfect but I don't think I was really bad.

I lost my temper sometimes, and there are times that you have to be harsh, when you run a business it's not like running a candy store or being somebody's maid. These people here didn't have the scope to be really bad. I did, but I did a lot of good, too. I gave lots to charity, plenty to the museums, the hospitals. There's a whole ward named for me and I'm on the Founders Wall in lots of places. I did plenty of good and I should enumerate those charities. They'll be impressed with what I did, I was no slouch, I sat on boards. What am I, chopped liver? Why should I be ashamed of how I lived? I was somebody, people were afraid of me. I'll be able to handle myself fine with the Court, no need to be too worried. But I better prepare, not take any chances. I'll cultivate this Malakh, he could prove useful, I'll throw him a couple of compliments, be friendly. You never know, his help might make the difference. Malakh reappears. This time he is bathed in light, horns of light seem to emanate from his face and form, and for the first time I notice that his facial features are different from ours, they are more diffuse, more vague. And yet, he is perfectly recognizable to me; but the light around him now makes it difficult to keep looking straight at him.

"Ladies and gentlemen," he announces, "I have just returned from the Higher Sphere and have in my possession a suggested schedule for each of you. Typically, our time together lasts for what you humans would call seven days, after which your souls migrate through the judgmental phase of thirty days. Sometimes these time periods are shortened or lengthened when circumstances dictate but I don't see any likelihood that your cases should require that. Our time together will be aimed at helping each of you inspect and evaluate your lives and in seeking for each soul a justification for your earthly existence. This justification, this argument, will then be presented by you to the High Court.

"Over the course of centuries, I have found that groups of souls who are processed together can assist tremendously in helping each other become aware of aspects of their lives which otherwise might be overlooked. Here there should no longer be any shame, no need for privacy. Each of your souls can help each other examine your lives without rendering judgment, helping only by singling out those moments in life that were positive, that could help in the Court. Each of you should know that there is a judgment and there is a Judge. And each of your souls will stand alone for that judgment, the most important moment in your existence, and you will be quite alone. You will be able to look back at your lives, to revisit certain moments if necessary. I will do my best to guide you, but at the end of the process you will stand alone."

I have to know more, I can't stand all this vague stuff. Judgments, High Court, it sounds silly. If there is a God, He knows everything, so what's the point? One, two, three, He knows what we are and what to do to us. What's this for?

Clarissa is no dope. Before I can ask, she does.

"Malakh," she asks, "if God is all knowing, He knows every little thing about us, even our thoughts. So why should we have to do this? What's the point?"

"She's right," I chime in. "There's something fishy here. Why dredge up all our actions when all is known? What's going on here?"

"Calm down, relax," suggests Malakh. "God doesn't need you to do anything. *You* need to do it, *you* need to make sense out of your lives. What egos you humans have, I'm always surprised. Little bags of wind, frail creatures, but, boy, what egos. You better take a deep breath, go with the flow here; you're not in charge here, you're not in control. Trust me, I'll guide you well."

"Why?" I counter. "What's in it for you? Why should you care about us, you don't even know us."

"It's my nature, that's the way we angels are made. Believe me, I wish I could stop caring, but I can't help it. We call it the 'angel's curse' up here. No matter how difficult or obnoxious or sometimes just plain dumb the souls are, we care. It wears us down. How much can an angel take?"

Essie speaks up. "Why, praise the Lord, I bless you for that. You're kind, a good angel, and I always felt surrounded by good angels, all my life. We're just scared here. We're all shaken up; this dying thing is new to us. You're a holy man, a holy thing. Don't get angry at us, we're doing the very best we can."

Clarissa also placates him. "Please bear with us, we're only trying to understand what's happening to us. I can see that you are a caring and kind angel, and I have every intention of following your lead."

Boy, is she good, she must have been a very successful personal shopper. Malakh is beaming, he bought it. I'll keep my mouth shut, leave it to the ladies. Women know how to handle a man, even an angel. Mendel winks at me, he understands the game now, too. On the other hand, Brett strikes me as a real shnook, an innocent. He looks about in awe; when Malakh looks his way he looks down, away, he doesn't meet the angel's gaze. I feel sorry for him, he's just a kid.

Clarissa is not finished with Malakh. I'm beginning to respect her, underneath that pretty decorated look lies a tough nut.

"With the utmost respect," she begins, "I understand that there should be no shame now, no embarrassment, but do we really have to reveal our secrets to each other? I mean, I never shared any of them with anyone, certainly not with my husbands or with my daughter. And I'd rather not have to relive some of what I went through with my first husband. Why should I share this with strangers? I don't even remember all the stuff I went through. You've heard of repression, I'm an expert. I don't want to revisit all that. And my business, all those spoiled and boring women whom I shop for, all that money and no taste, the bloody ones who spend weeks looking for a special outfit and then return it because they changed their minds on a whim. I lived through it once already, once should be enough. Can't we talk about pleasant things, crack a couple of jokes, wax nostalgic? After all, it's over, it's all over. Let them worry down there; we've suffered enough. Don't we deserve a rest?"

Malakh replies. "This is not a club, this is not a social event. We've got work to do and limited time in which to do it. We're short on angels, not enough to go around. I complained to one of the archangels but there's nothing he can do. It takes light-years to create angels and meanwhile souls keep on appearing, no end to them. And I understand

your desire for privacy, but I can assure you that the benefits of sharing your life information will outweigh the nega-
tives. It's important that you open up, talk your heart out.
You have to sum up your life. It's like a trial run, you're
preparing for the ultimate Judgment. You're rehearsing.
The Court wants to hear your version, to judge your character. You need each other, you'll help each other. My suggestion is that you begin, Clarissa, you or Essie. Women are
better at this than men, you'll set the tone."

Part II

Lives

"What kind of detail do you want?" Clarissa inquires. "Do I have to talk about sex, about money? What?"

"Tell me your life story," Malakh suggests. "Tell it the way you want to; I'm not editing. From time to time I may interrupt, I may conjure up flashes of your life visually. Be aware that past, present, and future are earthly ideas; here there is no real difference, we can jump back and forth with ease. Look, begin speaking and I'll guide you if necessary."

All eyes are on Clarissa. Her expression is serious now, wary.

"I was born in New Canaan, Connecticut, on—do I have to mention my age?—not quite sixty years ago. My parents were John and Betty Rivers; he was a banker, my mother was a housewife. They're both gone now, you didn't process them I suppose, Malakh; they died in Connecticut. I imagine we would have been described as upper middle class, although I don't remember realizing it until I went off to college at Briarcliff.

"I had everything I wanted as a youngster and so did all my friends, a nice home, cars, vacations. And I was a pretty girl, long dark hair, good figure, what my mother used to call 'cornflower blue' eyes. I was even a fairly good student, although no one seemed to care. There were plenty of boys, always loads of them, and I fully expected to marry one of them soon after school, have children, and live happily ever after. Amazingly enough, most of my friends did exactly that, and I don't know about the 'happily' part but most of them stayed married ever after. Not me. However, I did meet my first husband, Tommy, in our country club. He had graduated from Yale, his family was well known, not rich exactly but genteel, and he was working on Wall Street. Mr. Perfect."

A picture appears like a giant movie screen. A very young Clarissa in her wedding gown, holding a bouquet of white orchids.

"There are my parents," she exclaims. "Look how happy they were, look at my dad's face. My mother is wearing her mother's diamond earrings; those were only brought out for state occasions. There's my maid of honor, Lila. I haven't seen or heard from her in years. God, look how young we were, children really. And we were innocent, sounds silly today, but we were babes in the woods. Oh, the music—the processional is beginning."

And indeed we watch the ceremony; the old stone church with its vaulted ceiling provides the perfect setting, the music reverberating against its walls. Flowers along the aisle and surrounding the pulpit. Hundreds of guests in their finery, and, standing at the altar, her Mr. Perfect, tall, fit, fine-looking. As Clarissa is handed over to him by her father, the music and the picture begin to fade.

"Wait, oh, wait," Clarissa says, "oh, please, just another minute. Let me look one more time at my father. He died so soon after the wedding, just three months later. Look how well he looked then. I'd forgotten how happy he was on that day. He didn't say much, but his expression said it all. Malakh, just another minute."

The picture focuses in on her father as he smilingly steps away from the altar and then it freezes. Clarissa is still; a minute or so passes and the image fades.

"Okay," prods Malakh. "Let's continue."

"I was a virgin—par for the course in those days—and I remember how scared I was as we flew to Bermuda for our honeymoon. Very romantic, the Elbow Beach Hotel, music in the evenings, flowers everywhere, chocolates on our pillows every night. And Tommy did try, he really did. He was such a nice boy and he tried so hard, although I suppose *hard* is not quite the right word, but even now I can't understand how he could have gotten married to me, or anyone, if he couldn't, you understand, if he couldn't . . . do it. I don't want to say it out loud, you know what I mean. He was twenty-four, what did he think, the ceremony would help, the marriage certificate?

"And boy, did we try. I'll never forget lying there, the air conditioning so loud, the beautiful room with the water view and Tommy trying, trying and failing, night after night. He blamed it on the tension, the excitement, he pleaded for time. Toward the end of the week I became inventive, I tried some things I had read about, things the other girls had talked about. Believe me, I did my best but to no avail. Limp is limp. I must say that the days were fine. We swam. Tommy was great at tennis, at golf, at conversation. The nights, of course, were hell, but I figured that when we got back home, when we were both more relaxed, it would be all right, he could see a doctor, it would work itself out. And of course it did not.

"We had this wonderful little apartment on the Upper West Side of Manhattan, in an old prewar on West End Avenue. Tommy would come home late—he worked like a demon. And I always had a lovely little dinner prepared, just as I had been taught, the perfect little housefrau. We would chat, we never fought, not even once, and we never did you-know-what, not even once. Not even close. We tried wine, marijuana, even some rare herbs which could only be bought in Chinatown. I think they were mixed with rhino horns or something, they were supposed to create an erection. But the only thing that ever stood up was one of us, giving up and leaving the bed. And I really think Tommy began to hate me, or dread me at least. He came home later and later from the office. Of course, I knew he was not cheating—that was quite clear—but I was lonely. I even began to fantasize about our night elevator man, who was brazen enough to leer at me from time to time; at least I think he was leering. His English was poor and I didn't know a word of Croatian, but when I found myself mentally undressing him I knew I had to do something about my marriage.

"It was then, I think, that I began to shop rather constantly. We weren't rolling in money but Tommy never said a word when he saw the bills. I suppose he felt guilty, although when I bought my very first alligator handbag he did mumble something or other. The second and third just slid by and he never commented on the jewelry—not diamonds or anything too extravagant, you know, just gold. But I found a real consolation in buying beautiful things; there began to be a wonderful physical sensation when I found what I wanted, a subtle but persistent thrill, and then a moment of memorable pleasure when I paid and whatever I had bought was mine, all mine, mine alone. Sometimes my knees would tremble, I would feel flushed. I'll never forget my first ostrich-skin bag, it was bright yellow. I remember actually feeling faint at the moment of purchase. Only the fact that they did not have matching shoes in my size saved me from a crescendo of joy which would have, I'm sure, knocked me unconscious.

"And then I discovered Bergdorf Goodman, I had always hesitated to shop there, it's so high-end I was afraid to go inside. But once, I was caught in a rainstorm near the Fifty-eighth Street entrance; I *had* to go inside. Oh, the feeling, the happiness I felt, the endless possibilities, the sheer grandeur of it all. Believe me, no man I've ever known could possibly do for me what Oscar de la Renta can do with one flick of his wrist. Not to mention Bill Blass. When I think of him I call him Billy Boy, that's my private name for him; concentrating on his genius helped me through my divorce, because two years into my marriage Tommy and I were divorced. I never told anyone except my mother the real reason, never.

"You know, the amazing thing is that I bumped into him about five or six years ago, and he was still so handsome, and he was married. Married. I wanted so much to know what happened, was he able, but I obviously couldn't ask. I wonder if I should have hung in there, maybe it would have helped, who knows, but I was so young, what did I know? Anyway, that was marriage number one. My God, except for my mother, as I said, I never told this to anyone and yet it's spilling out of me; it feels so good just to say it, to unload it. None of you knew him, I didn't even mention his last name. Please don't think badly of him, we were so young and innocent. Anyway, that's what happened. That was my marital debut."

Brett speaks up, I'm surprised. "I think it was wonderful of you to keep that in confidence all this time. I really admire that, you could have been angry, you could have felt wronged. It was nice of you."

"Yes," says Essie, "he's right. The Lord should bless you

for that, you forgave him and we all need to be forgiven. Praise the Lord."

I don't know, I guess they're right, but I don't get it. How could a twenty-four-year-old man not know that he had this problem? It didn't dawn on him? I don't think I can remember too many twenty-four-year-old male virgins in my day. The guy was a *putz*, a fool, why shouldn't she have been angry? It screwed up her life, or could have. So I ask her.

"Clarissa, you mean to say that you never hated the guy? He could have ruined your life. You must have felt angry. Come on."

She looks at me intently. She's thinking, straining to remember. Finally, "No," she says, "no, I felt like it was my fault, maybe it was me. No, I was never angry at him. I was crushed, it hurt, but I never blamed him. I loved him. And I often think that the shopping expertise developed during that time in my life has added greatly to the richness of my life. Had I been busy raising children at that stage I might not have discovered the joys of the discerning shopper's eye, the qualitative differences in shoes and handbags, the subtleties surrounding the choice of just the right scarf, the right accessory. So I owe that in good measure to Tommy's lack of performance. Some good came out of it after all, and if nothing else my resolve stiffened to always find a kernel of good in every situation. No, the answer is no."

I'm surrounded by a bunch of saints, everybody so sweet, so kind. I'm in big trouble, all these sweethearts and an Auschwitz survivor and then there is me, not so sweet and with no excuses. What are these people, nicer than me or just dumb?

Malakh speaks up. "Clarissa, thank you for speaking so honestly about a painful time in your life. This is exactly the kind of dialogue that I want to see evolve, helpful to you and to us all. Why don't you go on? This may help jog your memory."

And before our eyes, there is a vision of a young, beautiful Clarissa in what has to be Venice, the Piazza San Marco, the music playing, the banners waving, birds everywhere, and she's sitting at one of those cafes—it must be early evening.

"Venice," she says, "my beautiful Venice. What a time I had! My mother insisted I go after the divorce, for the whole summer. London, Paris, Rome, the works, and then Venice. And the shopping, oh God, the clothes, they were a great comfort to me. But I was just twenty-five and still a virgin, a reluctant one by then. I traveled with two friends who went home after Rome and I went on alone to Florence and to Venice."

And strolling into the café comes a young man, American judging by his clothing, and takes a seat at one of the tables next to Clarissa's. He looks her over appreciatively; she doesn't appear to notice him at all. He orders an espresso in English, his voice loud, come on, Clarissa, give the guy a break, he's staring right at you. You're alone, he's alone, we must be seeing this for a reason. And sure enough, she turns to him and says, "Espresso? It's pretty strong the way they make it here. Can you handle it?" He smiles, he reddens a little bit, but he's quick on the uptake. "You'd be surprised what I can handle," he says and now it's her time to blush. Dear God, when you're young it's all so exciting, so adventurous, but watching it now from this vantage point it's all so predictable, so inevitable.

Next to me Clarissa exclaims, "Frank, Frank Parente, how wonderful to see him again! He was my antidote, the antidote to Tommy. He was a medical miracle, prescribed just for me and delivered at the right time; twenty-two years old, a construction worker from Brooklyn on his first trip to Italy. Look at that face, I'd forgotten his face, how beautiful he was, like a movie star. Look at that smile, from ear to ear, so warm, such a great smile."

He was a good-looking kid, and no wonder he was smiling. I'd be smiling, too. His lonely days were over and he must have known it, sitting there, eyeing his prey, like a hungry lion looking at a nice fresh piece of meat.

"Frank," Clarissa is again rhapsodizing, "how could I forget that face? His body I never did forget. The two weeks we were together I really hardly saw Venice. I didn't even miss the stores, that wonderful glass, those beautiful gloves, not even Roberta De Camerino's boutique. It was mostly his hotel room. My God, what a man, a miracle. Mr. Not So Perfect, but what a man. He was Italian, but Italian-American from Brooklyn, three years younger than I. I think he cried when he left me. I'm sure I saw him cry. I know he did; he had to go home back to work, he worked for an uncle in the construction business. He hadn't gone to college, he was Catholic, he had no appreciation of style, everything was wrong between us, and he knew it. I was starry-eyed, I thought we'd get married but he knew it was the end. Besides which, I suppose to him it was just two great weeks in Venice, something to enjoy, and then forget about. When I got home, we did date sporadically but everything had changed; all our differences were so glaring, the way he spoke, even the way he ate, he had no table manners, he buttered whole slices of bread and shoved them into his mouth, it all felt wrong, it *was* wrong. But after him, I came alive, everything inside me had changed. I'll never forget those two weeks. I wonder what happened to him, is he still alive, is he well? I owe him a lot."

It's amazing what a little sex can accomplish; she came alive, she *owes* him yet! I must have done a lot of good deeds in my time, all those needy women I helped.

"He's alive, he's fine, the father of three daughters; he runs his own construction business in Queens," Malakh reports.

"Does he think of me, do you think he ever thinks of me, of that time together?"

Malakh shrugs. "That much detail I don't know, probably he does. But continue—you're now back in the U.S., living in Manhattan."

"Yes, my mother paid the rent. She felt I should live in the city, more men, more possibilities. I got a job in advertising, copywriting, through my father's friend. And I kept busy. It was a happy time."

"Here's a face you'll never forget," says Malakh, and we view a man probably in his early forties, a distinguished face, a dignified appearance, looks like an expensive lawyer, formal. Thin features, thin smile, thin body. Classy guy.

"Andy," she says warmly, "my husband, Andrew Bowen. That's what he looked like when I met him, a banker like my father but much more successful. I was twenty-nine. He seemed to me to be much more mature than most of the men I'd been dating, a world traveler, self-made, and strong-willed. It took me a couple of months to really appreciate him. He didn't excite me at first, he was so steady, so predictable. And so formal, almost old-fashioned. I once jokingly asked him if he wore his tie to bed. I didn't know the answer because he didn't take me to bed until we were engaged. Things were different in those days, but can you imagine? I was beginning to wonder if I had found another Tommy. When we finally had sex I remember my overwhelming sensation being one of relief. But he persisted and we were married two weeks after my thirtieth birthday. My mother said he was the best birthday present I would ever have and, boy, was she right."

As Andy fades away, Clarissa pauses, her expression clouded, her face troubled. We all wait but she remains silent. The silence lasts too long, it becomes awkward. Malakh prods her.

"I understand, Clarissa, this is the hard part, but that makes it essential to talk about it; it has to be faced."

"I want to talk about the good things first," she replies. "The kindness, the friendship between Andy and me, the wonderful home we have, the way we helped each other through the hard times, the deaths of our parents, the surgeries. I don't want that to be forgotten. When I decided to become a personal shopper because I wanted to accomplish something, Andy backed me up even though it was an imposition on him, making it difficult for me to join him on his trips. We didn't need the money but I needed the responsibility and he understood. I owe him so much and I love him."

Again, the silence, again becoming awkward. "Twinky," says Malakh, "talk about your daughter, Twinky."

"That's her nickname, everybody calls her that. Her real name is Betsy but when she was little she loved that song, 'Twinkle, Twinkle Little Star.' Over and over she'd sing it and her nanny started calling her Twinky and it stuck. She's an only child, married now to a lawyer, no children yet. A lovely young woman, the apple of Andy's eye. And I taught her everything I knew, she's a fashion plate, elegance personified. She can look around a boutique and in seconds she knows what to go for and what to reject. She has an eagle eye, it's one of my gifts to her."

Again silence.

"You must, Clarissa, you have to," Malakh says forcefully. "You need to say it, out loud, it needs to be said. There is no shame here, there is no forgetfulness. Say it."

But she can't, she obviously can't. I want to intercede, to defend her, she's obviously embarrassed. But the angel looks at me, his eyes flashing.

"Silence," he says to me, as though he knows my thoughts. "Silence," he repeats, "let Clarissa speak."

The moment hangs heavy. Clarissa looks downward, avoiding our eyes.

"Andy and I had difficulty having a child, that's what you want me to talk about. We tried, the doctors could find no reason, we were each tested and retested, there was no reason discovered. It just didn't happen. I won't bore you with the particulars, the injections, the implantations, the tension. It was hard enough on me but it was impossible for Andy. The mechanics of it, the end of spontaneity, he found it all gruesome, humiliating. We did try and in the end he sat me down and we had it out. He wanted no more of it, he had had it. That's it, he said, if God doesn't want us to have a child, there's a reason and I accept it. No more, he said, we'll just do what comes naturally and whatever happens, happens. Or doesn't. And I agreed, I completely agreed. That was six years into our marriage. I was thirty-six. In those days that was pretty much the end of the line. The truth is, the spontaneity never really came back; there was little joy left in our sex life, not that it was ever very spectacular, something had gone out of it but that was okay. We had everything else and were fine. Please, why is it necessary to continue? What good will it do for these people to know anything more? Why must I do this?"

A visual emerges quite clearly. It seems to be a summer day; Clarissa is lying on a chaise near a swimming pool. The pool is surrounded by a wrought iron fence covered with foliage and bordered on one side by a small pool house with a striped green and white awning. Clarissa is reading a book, occasionally sipping from a bottle of water placed on the stone floor. The bucolic silence is suddenly interrupted by the arrival of a small van driven by a young man who opens the gate and enters the pool area armed with cleaning paraphernalia. A sandy-haired, pleasant-faced young man, well built, wearing a bathing suit and flip-flops and a baseball cap. He does a double take when he sees Clarissa. "Sorry, Mrs. Bowen," he says, "I hope I'm not disturbing you, but would it be all right to clean the pool now? It'll only take fifteen or twenty minutes."

"Of course, come right in, no problem," she replies, "and Don, please remember to turn the heat up again when you're finished."

He nods and goes right to work and Clarissa keeps an eye on him, even though the book remains upright in her hands. She's watching him as he goes about his work, she's watching him furtively as he bends over, his young and fit body on display. I know the look, hard to believe, but women used to look at me that way forty years ago and I still remember. She's got the hots for the kid, she must be well in her thirties but it's obvious. So this is what she's been hesitant to talk about, give me a break, one little scandalous affair. Wait until she gets a look at my life; whatever she did with this Don is peanuts compared to me. I don't even remember half of their names, I wonder if I ever knew some of their names. Much ado about very little here. I've got the feeling she's making too much out of some little peccadillo.

"Please understand," Clarissa says to us, "even looking back at this, knowing it happened, I still can't believe it. It wasn't just the sex; I was so depressed, so bored. And this boy came once a week. I would find myself waiting for him, managing to be around when he arrived. Even shopping had paled by then, nothing excited me. It must have been his youth, the idea that someone young and handsome might want me. I don't know, I don't even think I want to know. It probably would have come to nothing if he hadn't cut his damned finger."

The scene we've been watching has an audio.

"Shit!" yells Don. "Shit, I've cut myself. Damn it, there's a sharp edge on the end of the faucet. I sliced my finger."

And he has, it's bleeding.

"Dip it in the pool, the chlorine will clean it," Clarissa yells, "and I'll get the first aid kit. Come into the pool house."

And she rushes into the pool house to grab some Bacitracin and Band-aids. So this is what broke the ice, the kid got lucky and cut himself and nurse Clarissa is obviously going to dress his wounds and undress him. It's as clear as day, this must be Clarissa's big secret. We watch her carefully, ever so carefully, wrap up the kid's finger. He looks pale, she looks sympathetic. She gently strokes his arm, then his shoulder. He looks less pale, she looks very sympathetic. This is going to be fun to watch if Malakh lets us. Don looks into Clarissa's eyes, and she returns his gaze. Her hand is now on his chest. I'm rooting for him.

"You look pale," Clarissa says to him. "Why don't you lie down on the chaise. I'll get you some juice from the fridge here. Sit back, you'll feel better."

She grabs the juice and brings it to him. He takes a good drink of it, sits up straight, and puts the glass down. He looks directly at her, takes her hand, and pulls her toward him. The kid's a pro; this is not his first poolside adventure, he's in charge. And, just at the divine moment, wouldn't you know it, the visual fades, the last thing we see is his face buried in her breasts. My luck.

"All right," Clarissa says, "I suppose you've all guessed what happened next. I don't have to go into the gory details but that boy and I became lovers that afternoon, on the sofa in the pool house. Not very comfortable but very, very comforting and very, very different from what I had become accustomed to. And very, very guilt-ridden, too. I hate to admit it but that adds some spice as well. Six weeks of it, several times a week, you know what a nineteen-year-old boy can be capable of. Well, a thirty-seven-year-old woman can be even worse. Thank God that he had to go back to school. We never did it again after that summer; the next summer he did not reappear, but by then, anyway, I was nursing my child, possibly his child, although I was not sure, am not sure. Malakh, tell me, was he Twinky's father? He had to be, didn't he?"

Malakh nods affirmatively.

"What was his exact last name?" asks Clarissa, "Was it Berksman, what was it?"

"Berkson."

"Right, Donny Berkson. My God, Twinky's father. Is he alive? What does he do?"

"He's a tennis pro, lives in Tampa. Divorced, one daughter."

There's a question in all of our minds, the obvious question with an obvious answer. She never told her husband, good old reliable Andy; she couldn't have told him, she wasn't really sure herself. So Andy's "apple of his eye" is not even his own flesh and blood.

I can't resist asking. "Is Twinky good at tennis?" That was nasty, I'm going to be punished for that one, I'm going to fry. Why can't I keep my mouth shut?

"She's great at it, she's one of the best at our club," she says, her expression a mixture of pride and consternation. "Of course, she would be, wouldn't she?" she adds, grudgingly.

Essie speaks up. "Tell me, dear, did you ever tell your husband? He doesn't know, does he?"

"No, I couldn't. I don't know how he would have reacted and as time went by I realized that it was an isolated event. It never happened again, never came close. Why should I ruin everything, possibly break up our marriage, over a madness that I can't explain and over something I've felt miserable and guilty about ever since? And particularly when I saw the joy that the pregnancy brought to Andy, his pride, his happiness. It would have been cruel to tell him and, anyway, I wasn't really sure, was I? And I don't regret that decision, not for a moment. Maybe I'll be punished, but I don't regret it. I made Andy happy, he's a great father, what harm did I do him? I'll take the punishment. I think I made the right decision."

"We have a forgiving God," says Essie, "a forgiving Savior."

Maybe, I think, and how convenient that is. You poke around with some nineteen-year-old for weeks, foist your kid on your husband, and do it all for Andy! How touching. And her savior should forgive her. Maybe. I sure hope so because I would like to apply for all that forgiveness that Essie is so sure of. Essie probably never did anything that needs any forgiving, what the hell does she know?! This Clarissa, however, I like her. She had the good sense to have her fun and then feel guilty afterward, perfectly sensible. After-the-fact guilt was my specialty; luckily, it never hit early enough to ruin my plans. Too bad Clarissa and I didn't meet while we were alive, we both might have had quite a story to tell.

Malakh solicits our opinions. "Anybody want to express any reactions?"

"'Though your sins will be red as scarlet, I will forgive them'; it says that in the Bible," responds Essie.

Mendel chimes in. "I studied that in Hebrew when I was a child in Europe; that comes from Isaiah. I still remember it. We had to memorize it."

He mumbles something in Hebrew and then he translates.

"'Though your sins be as scarlet, they shall be as white as

snow.' But in the real world, punishments are given, terrible ones. Maybe first a person is punished and only then there is forgiveness. Who knows? This world is a swamp, who can figure it out? Don't worry, lady, what you did looks to me like a little button, a little crumb. I think on the scales of justice it wouldn't weigh much. Don't worry, it's a little pebble, not a stone."

Brett recites the obvious pablum. "You did what was best for your child. Who could blame you for that?"

Brother, what a sap. But I better not say too much, all this sweetness and light and I'm in a feisty mood. Look, I don't expect to get off scot-free but I make Clarissa look like Little Bo Peep.

"Line up behind me, Clarissa," I say, hoping to inject a little humor here. "Step behind me. When they finish hearing about my sex life they'll think you died a virgin."

Nobody laughs, although Clarissa does give me a little smile.

"I did it for Twinky and for Andy. I did what was best for the two people I loved most."

And at that instant we view her husband, older now, and her daughter, who must be in her twenties, and a young man who must be either the son-in-law or the boyfriend, all seated in the back of a limousine speeding along a highway. The young fellow holds Twinky's right hand while she leans against her father to her left.

"Mom would have been proud of the way you spoke, Twinky. It was a beautiful eulogy. I'm very grateful. And what a crowd, everybody from the club, everybody showed up. Everyone was so shocked, such a pointless death. There was a lot to look forward to, now nothing. It's unbelievable."

Twinky responds by squeezing his arm, says nothing.

"People will be coming by. I had Milly order enough food and wine, and I limited visits from six to eight in the evening, tonight and tomorrow. Afterward, next week, I'd like you to sort through Mom's things. Anything you want, jewelry, anything. Take what you want, the rest I'll let the family go through."

Clarissa stirs next to me.

"Oh no!" she exclaims. "My things, my bags, my jewelry, my furs. My collection, my Hermes, my Chanel. My God, he's going to let Nadia, that warthog of a sister of his—she never said a kind word to me—and her two dumpy daughters go through my things. Twinky better take my bags, my Hermes skin bags. She better not leave them for those women, it would be like throwing pearls before swine. And my emerald green bag, you know how hard that is to find, I bought it on Sloane Street in London, saved the V.A.T. And the orange one, I don't think there are more than two or three in the world in orange. Oh God, Twinky, don't leave that one. The alligator ones she can sell on eBay if she doesn't want them. And I never showed her the new beige goatskin one; I wonder if she'll understand how rare it is. My pearls, the giant South Seas, she won't leave those behind, and my diamonds are in the vault. Thank God for that. Whatever Twinky doesn't take that Nadia will grab. Not that my clothes will fit her, she's huge, a behind like an elephant, and who cares if she grabs my furs, she'll look like a bear cub in them. But I pray that the rest stays in the family. Years of shopping would go to waste if that great blob of a Nadia gets her paws on my things. Life is certainly not fair, but there should be a limit, and having her and her spawn parade around in my things would be well beyond all the red lines."

In the limousine, Andy turns to his daughter.

"You know what moved me most today, sweetheart? Not just your words, but the way you looked today, just like your mother years back. The same expressions, the way you carry yourself, every little detail. Her sweet, generous nature, her love of beauty. She lives on through you, she really does."

"Daddy," she replies, "we'll get through this. Blake and I will be there for you. It's unbearable, but we will bear it. I know I can because I'm *your* daughter, too. I've got your strength, I've got your toughness; people like us can get through whatever we have to. You're not alone and you won't be alone, I promise."

The guy is moved, his face crunches up in an attempt to

mask his emotions. He says nothing, he's busy holding back the tears. Maybe Clarissa is right, maybe she did the right thing.

As the moment fades away, Clarissa looks at us with a look of vindication.

"There it is, all the proof I need." She adds, "It's as clear as day."

"You didn't do it for yourself?" Malakh asks her with a rhetorical note in his voice. "Not even a little bit for yourself? This is the time for truth. There is no forgetfulness before the High Court, there is only truth. I want the truth to come out, otherwise the Court will be displeased. All your life you seem to have depended on others for your happiness, for your vindication, first your parents, then your husband, who seemingly was willing to support your shopping obsession. They set your standards, they made you happy. In almost every vital area. And then you meet a boy, seduce him, and have his child and raise her as your husband's daughter. You wanted your husband to continue to be your provider, your support. Do you really think of yourself as unselfish? You did this for him, not for yourself? I don't want your answer now, I want you to be ready when they ask you this in the Court on High. Be ready with the truth, Clarissa, be prepared. For now, you have said enough; study your own soul now, make your own judgment. I am not your judge but you will stand before Him soon. Be ready."

"That's the way you speak to her?" thunders Mendel. "She opened her heart to you and to us and you speak to her so? Is this right? Aren't you an angel, mister, aren't angels kind, or are you like people? This is the way to talk? The woman did one bad thing, maybe, who knows? Maybe she shopped too much, what do you expect, she's a woman. And you scare her this way? I saw babies taken by their legs, little ones, and dashed against the wall, their brains splashing out. I saw women and children herded into gas chambers, surrounded by German soldiers with clubs and with dogs. And you think her few weeks with some boy is a sin? Or maybe she spent too much at Saks? Where have you been? What world have you been dealing with? You should comfort her, not speak so harshly to her. Believe me, lady, it's all right, you'll be all right. You'll see your parents soon, don't be afraid. This Malakh of ours, don't let him scare you. Stick by me, lady, don't be afraid."

Malakh seems offended.

"What did I do?" he responds. "What, are you crazy? I wasn't mean, I warned her to be completely truthful, to be ready for the Court on High; truth is everything there, honesty is everything. Clarissa, I didn't mean to frighten you, believe me, that was not my intent. There are angels who do that, but I do not. He's right, Mendel is right, don't be afraid, you were a decent person. I just want you to be ready. I know what you are feeling, I told you, I also must face judgment once a year, I also must pass before the Judge's throne—and each and every year. You only have to do this once. Don't be afraid, but don't lie to yourself, either. Be honest."

"Honesty? You want honesty, mister, from me you'll get it," responds Mendel, on a tear now. "Whenever you're ready, I'll give you honesty. Now, you want? Here it is, I am Mendel, the son of Abraham and Gita Perlow of the city of Gyor in Hungary. My parents and my baby sister, Leah, and I were taken from our town with many others to Auschwitz in 1944. We went by train, in freight cars, no food, no water, standing, shoved in, worse than cattle. People died standing there, people froze, some went mad. Maybe they were the lucky ones. That you shouldn't show these people here, no pictures of that, please. Nobody should see such a picture, not down in that world, and not here. Skip the trains, my dear angel, even you shouldn't look at such a sight. Why don't you show them what it was like before the Germans came, how we lived. I would like to visit it again myself. Sometimes I think it was only a dream, that family, that home, maybe I only imagined it, because like a dream it flew away."

Spread before us is a family scene, a simple whitewashed room, a table laden with food, bread covered with a cloth, two candles burning. And a fragrant cooking smell, wafting over us, the smell of fresh bread, spices. A glass decanter of red wine surrounded by small cups. I recognize it immediately, it's a Friday night Sabbath table, like my grandparents had, the same look, the same smells. The two loaves of challah bread. But this room is a little fancier than in my family's apartment; there are drapes on the windows and the tablecloth is snowy white. Before I can comment, Mendel does, "It's *Shabbos*," he says, "my father's house. My mother made those drapes, her hands were magic, she could do anything. Can I see my family, Malakh? Let me see them, I have no photos, nothing was left to me, let me see them."

A dark-haired woman dressed in a dark-blue long dress bustles into the room, carrying a covered dish. "Leah," she calls, "Papa and Mendel will be back from *shul* any minute, are you ready?"

She's speaking in what I suspect is Hungarian, but I can understand every word and I see that the others do, too.

A little girl's voice. "Did you light already, Mama, is it *Shabbos* yet?"

"I lit the candles, it's already *Shabbos* for ten minutes. They'll be home soon, come down and help me."

A little girl, six or seven years old, rushes into the room.

"Get the horseradish for the fish," says Mendel's mother. "Put it in the glass bowl and get a spoon."

The child rushes out, excited to help.

"Leah," Mendel says, next to me. "It was before the enemy came, we were still in our home. I was still religious, or pretending to be, going to synagogue with my father, must have been at least a year before the Germans. Because already when I was fifteen, not later, I rejected all this ritual, the endless prayers, all the rules, *no* to this on *Shabbos*, *no* to that. I threw it all away, I was already a rebel at fifteen. So this was earlier, before I broke my father's heart, because I did break it. I was a tough number, a Socialist already at fifteen. How we fought, how we argued. And my poor mother, trying to keep the peace. My father, he was tough, too, but not tough enough to convince me. The endless praying, all the rules, it was not for me."

We all watch as a young Mendel comes into view, accompanied by his father. "Good *Shabbos*," says the father, a bearded man in his forties, a sturdy man dressed in a black suit and a black hat, his arm around Mendel's shoulders. He kisses his wife and catches his little girl with his free arm as she returns his greeting.

Next to me, Mendel says, "Enough, enough. Please, no more. Look at me, I must have been fourteen there, maybe already fifteen, look at me. You can already see in my face, in my expression, what was brewing. Many of my friends, too, were filled with the new ideas, the whole world was simmering with new ideas. I don't want to see anymore now. If I had known what was coming, the Germans, the murderers, if I had any idea, I would have shut my mouth. But who knew, who could imagine? I made my father very unhappy, every *Shabbos*, every holiday, the arguing, the yelling. And once I'll never forget, once I went too far, it was at the Passover Seder. I made fun of the story, what, I should believe that 650,000 slaves left Egypt and lived on manna in the desert? 'Nonsense,' I said. 'Maybe the whole story is nonsense.' My father didn't argue, not that time. He just looked at me with such a sad look, like he had lost all hope. His whole body sagged. He slumped down in his chair and looked intently at me. Finally he asked, 'Do you believe in nothing?' 'Nothing,' I confirmed, 'zero.' There was a painful silence and then he began to lead the Seder again, on and on he went and I knew that I had broken his heart. And also mine, my heart, too. I don't want you should show anymore, I remember very well. I only wanted to see their faces once more, still in our own home, before the world burned."

Brett interjects. "Mr. Perlow, please don't feel so bad about your behavior. Every boy rebels against his father, every normal boy. If not in one way, then in another. And the closer the two are, usually the bigger the rebellion. It was normal. If the Germans hadn't come it would have blown over, you and your father would have laughed about it."

"Sure," I agree, "it's perfectly normal, Mendel. He's right."

Mendel doesn't even acknowledge our comments. His thoughts are elsewhere, far away.

"When the Germans came for us, when they emptied the ghetto and forced us onto the trains, I watched my father, I watched him as they packed us in. How could he believe? But he did, he went onto that train believing; he left that train in Auschwitz still believing. After we arrived, quickly, before we could think, dogs were barking, we were being hit by rifle butts and by whips, we were separated from my mother and from Leah right there on the platform. We soon learned that we would never see them again. And then came the labor and the starvation and the cruelty. My father began to fade away and over and over he would say to me, 'You are lucky, Mendel, we were taken late in the war, you will survive, you are young.' He would slip me an extra potato, a turnip, sometimes some soup—he was resourceful, my father. Only later did I begin to think that maybe it was his own food he was giving me. To this day I don't know, I don't want to know; was it his own food that he gave me? I was so hungry, I ate it, I never asked.

"Over and over, day after day, he would say that I must live and that I must say the memorial prayer, the Kaddish, over him when he dies. I didn't argue, I could see he was slipping away. Do you know he lived until nine days before liberation—nine days—that holy man. I don't know on what he lived, on the air maybe, or maybe out of love for me. And then he died; one morning he was dead, cold, lying next to me, his mouth open. I had to leave him there. One

had to be at roll call, no excuses, otherwise a bullet. At
night, he was gone, the body was gone. I tried to say the
Kaddish, but I fell asleep in the middle of it. Also the next
morning at roll call, I tried, I did some of it. To whom was
I praying, and for what?

"And then, a few days later, the Russians came. Every
once in a while I recited what I could remember of the Kaddish, in the hospital and afterward for most of a year, I did
sometimes say the Kaddish. And after that I never said
another prayer ever again, never. Not one. And I never will,
never. You want honesty, here it is. You are saying there is a
Judge, a God, and I don't even question it. So there *is* one.
But if He doesn't help, so what? Who cares? My sister was
eight years old when they killed her, my mother was not yet
forty. They were hurrying, the Germans, trying to kill as
many as possible before the Russians came. So now, tell me,
Malakh, for what should I have prayed? For what? For
mercy? What do you have to say, mister angel?"

"Mendel, what can I say? But let me show you the last
picture of your parents and of Leah, the one taken at your
aunt's wedding in Budapest in 1943. Let me do this for you;
here, Mendel, take a look."

A picture emerges, a formal picture—Mendel's father,
bearded and austere, his wife dressed in a long black dress
with rows of pearls around her neck, Mendel, big dark eyes
still recognizable, solemn-looking in the picture and, next to

the mother, the little girl, all dressed up with a bow in her hair, the same big dark eyes and a happy smile. The picture has a posed, artificial look about it, a period piece. We all look at Mendel, all eyes on him, as he stares at the picture.

"It's been so long," he says quietly, in a flat voice, hard to hear. "Look at my mama, so beautiful, a lady. And Leah, she would have been a beauty, too." No tears, not even a perceptible change of expression. But his voice, like a thin reed, weak. "Papa," he says, "I tried to say the Kaddish, I did the best I could. I hope you were satisfied."

We are all silent, none of us are foolish enough to speak. What is there to say?

"Will I see them?" asks Mendel. "Will I be able to see them again? I've grown old and they could not age, would they recognize me now? I look older than my age, an old man. How will they know me, Malakh, answer me, will I see them again? And my wife, will I see her?"

"It is possible; there are reunions of souls, but this is not my area. I'm not an expert. Please, I'm only able to guide you through this process, please don't ask me for more. I'm not certain of the answers, so much depends on the judgment. But Mendel, I hope that you will see them again and that to them you will seem as young as you were then."

The pain we have all seen has silenced us, even Malakh seems worn down. The silence grows and I begin to relish it, I'm okay with it. It's healing in its way.

Finally, it's Mendel who speaks. "More?" he asks, "you want more? Malakh, yes?" The angel nods, his expression neutral.

"Six months in a sanitarium in Switzerland. While the Germans were killing us, the Swiss borders were closed; they turned back Jewish refugees when they caught them. But after liberation, even they let some of us in and there I was being treated in one of their hospitals, clean, so sterile, everyone polite. And there I debated whether to try to get into Palestine, which the British were blockading, or to try to write to my mother's uncle who had moved to America before the war. But first I wanted to go home to Gyor; maybe somebody made it back, a friend, someone. That trip was arranged for me and I returned almost a year to the day from when we were deported. Some Jews had returned, one of my father's close friends made it, two of my cousins who had hidden in a nearby farm. Maybe sixty or seventy of us. The atmosphere was filled with hate, people were unhappy to see us, they had taken our property, our homes, our furniture, our shops. The air was thick with danger, there were cases of returnees who were killed. My parents' home was lived in by a family which had migrated from another town—they claimed that the house had been empty when they arrived. Nothing was as it had been and, as you know, I had not even a photo, not a letter, not a book left for me.

"When a letter arrived from my uncle in New York in

response to mine, I left Gyor and came to New York. I arrived by boat, I was numb, I remember very little of the trip, only the soup, wonderful soup every day and no limit to how much you could have. And on the pier, waiting, was my great uncle and with him his whole family, children, grandchildren, a whole army of people. Can you imagine? Nobody missing, generations of a family together. And then I really cried. I didn't cry in the camp, not for my father, my mother, Leah; there was no time, maybe that's why I didn't cry. I was half alive, numb. But when I saw that family, the children, the grandchildren, I couldn't speak. They were talking, patting me, hugging me, and I couldn't say a word. And then I began to cry; I didn't yell but I couldn't stop crying. All the way to Brooklyn, to their nice house in Boro Park, my own room, my own bed, and I cried. Sometimes I feel like I never stopped, not really, all these years, the store, my wedding, my son, my grandsons. Still, it feels like it was all in tears, everything."

But Mendel is not crying now as he speaks; his face is controlled, poker-faced.

Another picture appears. Must be his wedding. There he is in a dark suit, skinny and the woman next to him short, pretty, a little plump in her gown, both look very serious, solemn.

"No parents, no in-laws," says Mendel, "my wife, Luba, was also a survivor; hidden near Salant in Lithuania by her

nanny, she alone made it out of three sisters and two
brothers. She was blonde, like her mother, that helped. Her
cousin and my uncle sat side by side in the Boro Park synagogue and that's how we met, one, two, three, we married.
She was a very quiet woman, smart, never complained.
Without her, the store could not have been; she was my
partner, she shared all the problems. Only one thing she was
crazy for, my son, our only child, Abraham Zalman we
called him, after our two fathers.

"What she didn't do for him! The tutoring, we spent
blood money on those tutors, *kishke gelt*, money that we
needed for living. She moved heaven and earth for him.
She wanted him to be the best and he was, the best student, the best writer, he was even good at sports, that
baseball that they play here. And basketball, one of us
would go to every game he played in, the other one stayed
in the store. He's still the best, a partner in Wall Street now,
with a driver and a big sedan car and with a fancy wife,
butter wouldn't melt in her mouth, a cold fish. Luba didn't
live to see his big success but she wouldn't be surprised, she
believed in it, she made it happen.

"And we raised him right, we sent him to Hebrew School,
he had a Bar Mitzvah, not that you'd know it now, he's a
fancy man now. He calls himself Avery now, not Abraham,
Avery S. Perlow. At least, the Perlow he kept. I'm surprised
she let him, his wife, I'm surprised he's not a Per or a Pearl,

who knows, give her time. They live up in Connecticut, near where you come from, lady, in Greenwich. What a house. In Hungary only a nobleman lived like that, only a prince. They invite me for the holidays and I go, I see my two grandsons, with them I have fun. We see eye to eye, those boys and me. I tell them all the stories about the family, about Gyor, about the camp. I hide nothing from them, they'll remember their grandfather, they should know from where they came. They should be ready if it ever happens again."

"Would you like to see your son again, Mendel? After the funeral, he went alone to your apartment above the store, he went through your things. Here, I'll show you."

And an image appears, a man in his fifties; you can see the resemblance although he's much taller than his father, broader in build, thinning blonde hair, expensively dressed. He is dutifully going through every drawer, all the papers. Behind him a younger man in a dark suit, and a dark cap, probably his driver, is arranging what he is handed into cartons, which he seals and sets aside. Mendel's son finally seems to have finished; he holds a small book in his hands and instructs the driver to remove the cartons and to call Goodwill and arrange for the pickup of everything else. Alone now in the apartment, he sits wearily in an old armchair and leafs through the book.

Mendel is moved, I'm surprised to see how intently he watches his son.

"My memorial book," he whispers. "Years back I put down all I could remember of Gyor, the names, the people, what our home was like, everything. My experiences in the camp, how I tried to say Kaddish for my father and how often I failed. Everything is there. I spilled my guts into that book when Abe was born, I wanted him to know but I never succeeded to give it to him. I tried at his Bar Mitzvah but he never opened it, he was too busy. So I put it away, haven't looked at it in years. And now he reads it, what will he think? I never really told him how I hurt my father with the religion, how I fought him on that. I never explained. What will he think of me, why should he know such a thing? I should have thrown the book away long ago, better my son should think that I was a good son, that I honored my father."

We all watch Avery's face as he reads on. His cell phone rings but he does not respond. The muscles of his face betray the intensity of his concentration. After some time, he closes the book, picks up his phone, and dials a call.

"Bill," he says, "I'm coming down now."

He takes the book and walks wearily down the stairs to the street. He looks around and walks down the street to Fineman's kosher deli on the corner, goes in for a minute and checks where the nearest synagogue is, and then reemerges and enters the car. We watch him travel three blocks and stop in front of a small synagogue, which he enters. Some men are sitting in the chapel and he goes up to one of them, inquires when the afternoon service begins.

"As soon as we have a minyan we'll begin," says the man. "With you we're eight men, if two more don't show up soon we'll make some calls. What, you have Kaddish?"

"Yes," says Avery. "I buried my father this morning."

"This morning? Aren't you sitting shiva, why aren't you at home?"

"No, I'm not religious, not a member of a synagogue community. But I do want to say Kaddish, that I want to do."

"Sure, and what's your name?"

"My name is Abraham, Abraham Zalman, the son of Mendel Perlow."

"Mendel Perlow, your father was Mendel? A fine man. Not a believer, but when we needed a minyan, we would call and he would come. He wouldn't recite word one, but he would come to make the minyan. A good man, he should rest in peace."

Several more men file in and the service begins. At the appropriate minute, one of the congregants stands next to Avery and recites the Kaddish out loud with him, helping him through it. *"Yisgadal v'yiskadash shmei rabah. . . ."* On and on the solemn cadence of the prayer is recited and Mendel seems mesmerized, his gaze focused on his son. At the end of the short service, Avery turns to leave but the men surround him and each one repeats the same phrase,

"May God comfort you among the mourners of Zion and Jerusalem."

The picture fades but Mendel still stares at the place where it had been. After some time, he lifts his eyes and meets our gaze, he looks around at us all.

"He said the Kaddish for me," he says. "He remembered to do that. He said the Kaddish. And his name, they asked him his name, did you hear, Abraham Zalman, Abraham after my father and Zalman after Luba's. I must tell Luba. I'll tell her when I see her."

And Mendel begins to cry, to weep out loud. The wrenching sound of his sobbing leaves me feeling helpless. I just float there and watch. We all do; even Malakh is silent. Finally, the sobbing subsides, the crying stops, tears have a limit. After some minutes of silence, Malakh ventures to speak.

"Mendel, are you finished now? Do you want to say anything more? Or are you done?"

"Done, I'm done, don't you see, can't you see, I'm forgiven, my father has forgiven me, don't you understand. It's a sign, my father understands, he's forgiven me. I was young, you know what it is between a father and a son. The rabbis say that when the Messiah comes, fathers and sons will be reconciled, that's how hard it is to do, that's what it will take. But here it has been done, the circle is closed. So I'm done, I'm done, no more now, let me rest."

Essie agrees. "That was a sign from the Lord, all your memorial prayers were accepted and you are clean before the Lord, yes sir, clean and pure before Him. Praise be to God."

Clarissa adds, "I'm so happy for you, you should be proud of your boy."

Mendel makes no reply, his eyes remain closed.

"Let him rest," I suggest, "he needs to rest."

I'm happy for the old man, he seems to have reconciled his feelings. Good for him, he's been through enough. "You mentioned your relationship with your father, Brett, why not continue and talk to us about your life now?" invites Malakh.

"I'm not sure that some of you," and Brett glances at all of us, "will be receptive to my story, some of you may think less of me. I wonder if I could be exempted, Malakh. Maybe you and I could have a private conversation. I don't want to offend anyone, you're all such nice people. Perhaps you'll agree to let me speak privately."

"Look," says Malakh, "in the past few hours alone I've developed a backlog of souls that would cross your eyes. A murder victim, three innocent victims of gang shootings, and thirty-eight deaths from natural causes. All of them are in limbo, waiting for me. I've told you, we're short of angels, there's no time for private screenings. If you were really evil you wouldn't be here, you'd be in a completely separate process, much more rigorous. Nothing you've done is that out of the ordinary according to your case file. Please get started."

But Brett seems hesitant, he resists. "I don't know where to begin," he complains.

"You want me to jog your memory? You want a little visual help to jog your memory?" There is a threatening note in Malakh's voice, no more Mr. Nice Guy. "You want them to see your first night in your career as an interior decorator—shall we start there, you and your boss, remember? Or would you like to begin from the beginning?"

"Okay, all right, I understand. We'll start from my childhood. Don't be annoyed, please, Malakh, please let's do it chronologically. I was born in Akron, Ohio; my parents were solid, good people. My father, Doug, was a real American type, strong, tough, a policeman who rose to lieutenant, but full of street smarts. He met my mother, Mary, in high school, they married soon after graduation. He fought in Vietnam and was proud of his service, he was proud that he could support his family, that his wife could be a homemaker. Proud of his daughter, my older sister, Sally, and proud of me, until I left for New York. Then things changed, but that comes later. He was a principled man, a straight arrow, not much sense of humor, solid. My mother was kindness personified, selfless, also clueless about life, living in a pleasant little world of family and close friends. The farthest they ever traveled together was once to New York, after I moved there; my father felt he had seen the world while in the military; my mother had no real interest, she was perfectly happy in Akron."

And there it is, rising before us, a neat gray-shingled two-story house on a street of similar homes. Well kept, on a neat plot of land, flagpole in front, separate one-car garage to the side.

"Home!" exclaims Brett. "That's our home. There's Pete, my dog," as a collie ambles down the front steps, tail wagging, greeting a boy running up the front path. "Oh God, that's me, look at me, I must have been fourteen or fifteen. Jesus, look what I'm wearing, my camp shirt and shorts. It's the summer, I'm back from day camp, my mother will be waiting for me inside with Kool-Aid and some of her cookies. Just watch."

And we do. Brett enters the house, yells, "Mom!" and is answered, "In the kitchen." Sure enough, she's pouring something cherry red from a pitcher; cookies are piled on a plate on the table.

"How was camp?" she asks. "How was your day? You look pale, drink up, the cookies are fresh, just like you like them."

Good God, I'm thinking, take out the violins. Could be a *Saturday Evening Post* cover, with a collie yet. The kid's life story is going to put me to sleep, it'll be as exciting as watching flies fornicate. What could he have been thinking, pleading for a private session?

Well, here comes Dad, uniformed and sweaty. Mary rushes to the refrigerator, pours the returning hero a cold drink.

"Sally," she yells, "Daddy's home." Father and son exchange mock salutes. This whole scene could be a TV ad for Kool-Aid.

Next to us, Brett is moved, at least I think he is, his face flushes, his jaw clenches. Not exactly the expressive type but he is obviously moved.

"Look how handsome my Dad was, and tough. I never saw the man flinch, never. Nothing ever scared him, I swear I never saw him scared. Me, I'm scared of almost everything, almost everyone. Not him, not 'til the day he died. I don't know how he ever produced me, he must have wondered where I came from. They both must have."

"Why, Brett? I just don't understand," Clarissa interjects. "You obviously had a wonderful home, wonderful parents. What was wrong?"

"Please, ladies, Essie, Clarissa, please, you might not want to hear the rest. I'm not sure that you should."

"Oh, for God's sake, weren't you listening to my life? Who do you think I am, Mother Teresa? What are you afraid of?" asks Clarissa.

Essie is all kindness. "Lord have mercy, speak up, boy,

don't be afraid. This is the time for forgiveness, we all need
to be forgiven. Get on your knees before the Lord and con-
fess whatever it is and you'll be covered under the blood.
Yes, Lord, thank you, Jesus."

Mendel's eyes remained closed, there will be no comment from him. Everyone is looking at me. I don't really
give a damn what the story is, to tell the truth, but I've got
to be decent here. So I mumble some encouragement.

"Come on, Brett, we're all in this together. Spill the
beans, I'm going to, and believe me, I should probably be
more unhappy about it than any of you."

And we wait. Brett is trying, you can see that he's trying
to find the right way, the right words.

Malakh decides to move things along. It's a campsite that
comes up, tents, campfires, the silvery movement of a river
nearby, a moonlit night.

"Oh, no," says Brett, protesting, "that's not necessary. I
don't want to see that. Neither do they."

But the image persists.

"Okay, guys," says a counselor, "pair up, two to a tent,
fifteen minutes to lights out. Jackie, you share the tent with
the junior counselor; Brett, you can move into my tent. The
rest of you pair up and do it fast."

All right, now we know. The poor kid. Big deal, what was
he, fifteen? Even the counselor was a kid, probably a college
kid. It happens.

Thank God, the image fades. Looks like there's no catering to prurient interests up here; that's good for me when my turn comes. Less is more.

"I knew it was wrong, what happened," says Brett. "I was religious, I knew it was wrong. In the beginning everything was normal, he went to sleep, so did I. I was tired. I woke up with him on top of me, his hands all over me, his mouth on mine. I should have yelled, I should have fought back but I was scared, I was shocked. He was so heavy and he was the counselor so I just lay still. I don't remember what he did. I can remember his face, the expression on his face, and I remember the weight of him pushing the breath out of me. I don't know exactly what he did. But it went on and on. I don't even remember his name. I must have known his first name, but it's gone from my mind. The next night it happened again; it went on half the night. We never discussed it, not during and not after. And it never happened again, only on that sleepover trip, for the rest of the summer everything went back to normal. But for me, nothing was ever the same, not really. Was it because he did that to me, or maybe it was innate, there already? I don't know, but it never was the same for me ever again."

"You never told your parents, your teachers?"

This from Clarissa. Of course he didn't, how could a boy report that to his father? No way.

Brett nods in response. "No, not a word. And it didn't happen again until New York, although it was always on my mind. I tried with girls, twice, but it didn't work for me, it wasn't for me."

Brett pauses and we all wait for him to resume; Clarissa seems sympathetic, Essie a little wide-eyed. Mendel's eyes remain closed. I wonder if he's listening. I don't know what to think, I've never understood that whole thing. It seems to be inborn, genetic, although maybe an incident like that could bring it out. He's a strong, virile-looking kid, you would never guess.

A New York City scene appears, Manhattan, looks to me like the NYU neighborhood. Lots of college-age kids, crowds of them, books in hand. And there's Brett, dressed in black, waiting on tables in a little Italian restaurant.

"There I am," he exclaims, "waiting tables. I did that to help with my living costs; the scholarship wasn't enough. Boy, it was tough, the courses, the tests, and the weekends and two nights a week as a waiter."

"Didn't last long, did it?" prompts Malakh.

"No, no, it didn't; that's where I met Freddy, that's when everything changed."

"There he is," says Malakh, "entering the restaurant right now. Must have been a regular—the owner is dancing around him."

"Yes, he came in at least twice a week, always the same table and usually alone. He lived really close on Lower Fifth Avenue."

Freddy is a man in his late thirties or early forties, flamboyant—a beige scarf tied around his neck and flung over one shoulder of his expensive suit—a dandy. Something a little affected about him, hard to put your finger on. Handsome man, his hair perfectly combed, skinny and fit and very aware of the entrance he is making. He beams a warm smile at Brett, who stands in attendance. He places a hand on the boy's shoulder, gives him an exuberant greeting. Obviously he's the next chapter in Brett's little tale of woe. Okay, let's hear it.

"I've been giving you a lot of thought, Brett. I have an offer to make you," says Freddy. "After work tonight, can we meet? You know I run a decorating business, seven on staff and growing, and I'm always looking for new talent and I've had my eye on you for a while. Let's talk about it when you're free."

Brett replies, "Thanks, I'm really grateful, but I don't know much about decorating. In fact, I don't have any experience at all with it. I've never bought a piece of furniture, I'm living in a dorm. What use could I be?"

"I like to train young people, train them my way. I can tell from the way you conduct yourself that you are likely to have potential. You have a winning smile, a certain style about you, a flair. You would not be the first one I have seen potential in, and I could use you part time, you could work around your school schedule. Here's my home address. You get off here around ten o'clock, right? Come by at eleven, I'm up 'til all hours. We'll talk."

The spider and the fly, so what else is new? How many secretaries did I hire just that way? Remember Jean, I swear I don't think she could type, and that big beautiful one from Belgium, she didn't last very long, she hardly understood English.

An apartment comes into view, what a place, serious money was spent there. Now that's something I am painfully aware of, having lived through two decorating binges by Jane. Everything is beige, beige carpets, drapes, couches, the New York Beige look, we had that in our first co-op, courtesy of our decorator, Drake, that miserable money-grubbing, sneaky son of a bitch. He got his hooks into Jane; he just wanted to change the floor, he didn't approve of the wood color, he replaced it with stone, and then, lo and behold, once that was changed the walls needed to be painted a different color and the drapes clashed, they had to go. And the chandeliers, that miserable swindler called them "lights,"—that was the right word—the "lights" needed to be replaced. Color needed to be added, he wanted colored glass and he found just the right light, a massive one from Venice; antique, it had to be antique, anything else wouldn't have been good enough. Sixty-five thousand dollars for his damned light plus a third for him. I should have hanged him from it. I'm not fond of decorators and now I have to watch Freddy. What in God's name is he wearing? It looks like a T-shirt and shorts in some gold color but it is one piece. Must be his special interview outfit, he must do his interviewing in his underwear. Or maybe in even less. The doorbell rings, and Freddy pads barefoot across the living room through the gallery to the door. He glances in the hall mirror, pats down his hair, and then opens the door. And there's Brett. Come in little fly, the spider is dressed in gold, just for you.

"Wow!" exclaims young Brett, as he looks around in awe. "Everything is so beautiful. I've never seen a room like this, it's like a museum. Geez, I can't believe it. Can you really teach me how to do this? I'd love to learn. Everything is beautiful."

"Everything?" asks Freddy, preening. "Every little thing?" And he rests one hand on Brett's upper arm. "Me, too? You did say everything." Freddy flashes a wide smile at the boy.

We all see Brett's face, his expression changes, something dawns on him. He gets it, he finally understands. There's a quid pro quo here, my boy, no more shlepping trays, lots more money. The kid's getting it finally, a little slow on the draw but not totally dumb. I guess it is an important moment for him, a lot depends on what he does next. It's perfectly evident that he's tempted, he keeps on looking about, avoiding Freddy's gaze. Finally, he turns toward his host, looks directly at him, and surrenders.

"Everything," he replies. His shoulders sag a little, his face reddens. "Everything in this room is beautiful," he adds as he removes his jacket. That is clearly not all that is going to be removed tonight. "Of course, you, too."

"Make yourself comfortable; let me get you a drink, sit down and relax."

The picture begins to fade, the rest is commentary. We all turn and look at Brett; his expression betrays the seriousness with which he has viewed that moment in his life. "That was the beginning," he mumbles, "or maybe the end. From then on no monetary problems and I began to understand who I was, what I was. All those longings, those attractions, began to make sense. I guess I finally accepted the inevitable. And I was happy, really happy for some time. He was nice to me, and I learned a lot from him. I would go with him to the clients' homes, I would watch him operate—what a salesman he was. He taught me about colors and spatial relationships and I found he was right about me; it wasn't all nonsense, I really had some talent. He was a master at getting clients to spend their money, he wove a web of warmth and seeming concern, never forgot their birthdays and anniversaries. Little charming presents would descend on them from time to time, and he would keep up the charm offensive for years after a job was completed. 'You never know when and if the buggers will move or renovate,' he taught me, 'become their best friend, make them rely on your taste.'

"He would go on shopping trips with the wives overseas, London, Rome, all expenses paid; the husbands were generally happy to pay, they'd get a vacation from their wives and, God knows, Freddy was no threat. And you know what was magical about him, if an item came in wrong—wrong size, wrong color—he would spin a tale, he would change the error into a new design imperative, he would claim he had yielded to an irresistible impulse. 'Trust me,' he would say, and they did, they fell for it. Custom-made rugs that were mismeasured were hung as tapestries; he had one lady using a cracked Georgian chamber pot as a sink for her vanity; he told her that the crack gave the pot its character. When things got slow he would call one of the ladies, he had a dream, he felt the need for a change of art in their rooms, a fresh wind, a new aesthetic. And a hell of a commission.

"And I earned every penny he paid me. During the day I trolled around the wholesalers and antique shops looking for bargains, and at night I was on duty at least three or four times a week. Aside from his undignified habit of moaning and sometimes screaming out loud during our night sessions, it was pleasant enough, brief and to the point, and always the same. Oddly enough, he displayed very little imagination in bed, fifteen minutes work and he'd roll off me and go to sleep. After some time it was a bit boring but I was rolling in money, whatever I wanted, clothes, trips, and I did enjoy the sex."

Brett pauses and then with a perceptible note of regret, he continues. "And then came La Fefferbaum, that witch of a Fefferbaum, Gladys. She was maybe five foot two in her stocking feet and what feet they were, large feet, flat feet. And they were her best feature. Her father owned blocks of buildings in Soho, *blocks*, so she had endless gobs of money to spend. Freddy became her best friend; he would help her shop for her clothes, gratis. But nothing helped, because as she grew closer to Freddy she began to dislike me more and more. Maybe she was jealous, she was certainly mean and vicious. For months I took it, her nasty comments. She blamed everything on me. One of the rugs we custom ordered had came in from India with the wrong colors; that was my fault, too. 'The only reason Freddy keeps you,' she said to me with daggers in her eyes, 'is so he can drop something on the floor and enjoy watching you bend over to get it.'

"I begged Freddy to assign someone else to her project but we were too busy, it didn't happen. And I snapped; I admit it, I lost it. One horrible afternoon, I don't even remember what she was yelling at me about but she ended her harangue with the suggestion that she was tired of dealing with someone who spread his legs for a living. In retrospect, she was somewhat accurate but who the hell was she to say that. 'Mrs. Fefferbaum,' I replied, 'go fuck yourself and I certainly hope you do because no one else, living

or dead, would want to do it for you.' I have to admit that
the expression on her face was not compensation enough for
the aggravation that followed. Freddy was fond of me but a
lot fonder of commissions. My job teetered in the balance.
A number of extraordinarily creative nights, exploring new
ways to please Freddy, seemed to placate him. And then
came the drapes. The drapes are what did me in."

Here Brett pauses, he sounds annoyed.

"We were working on this huge job in Greenwich. Our
clients, the Cardins, had bought a sixteen thousand-foot
house, a palace, and Freddy was doing his beige thing.
Everything beige except for little accents here and there,
'color points,' he called them. It made our lives easy,
nothing clashed, and the Cardin woman was convinced that
Freddy was a genius. How was I to know that our drapery
supplier changed its color code? I never got any notice in
writing. So when Freddy told me to order number fifty-three
for the drapes—that would be his usual Champagne Beige—
I did it. Some simpering idiot at the drapers had changed the
color codes and I didn't check, why would I check? Twenty-
six rooms' drapes were involved. The order came to a hundred sixty-seven thousand dollars before our commission and
number fifty-three turned out to be Passion Pink, miles and
miles of lurid pink. Now Freddy did try to save the day. He
claimed a change of vision, an adventuresome touch. But
not even the Cardins could fall for that one. They sued

when Freddy resisted absorbing the mistake and they asked for damages. That was the coup de grace for me. It was also the end of my career as a decorator. Freddy ranted and raved, threw me out of his apartment, and threatened me with bodily harm. And worse, he blackballed me in the industry, pinkballed, I guess would be more accurate. I was unemployed and unemployable."

I'm beginning to like this kid, he's got some spirit, he's not what I expected. So I ask him, "What was your next gig, Brett?" He gives me a sardonic look.

"I was not anxious to go back to being a waiter, that was for sure. And I missed the sex, so I joined a gym. I wanted to keep in shape, and I awaited the inevitable response. Men approached me and I would go home with someone, do what comes naturally, and collect a few hundred dollars for doing it. I had one guy who visited me at least twice a week, two-hundred fifty dollars a session. All I had to do was play Cole Porter music and when the tune that begins 'Strange, dear . . .' came on, so would he. That went on for almost a year. I think I made more money from that music than Cole Porter ever did. And then there was Teddy—he was a big man, strong guy—just before the divine moment he would begin to sing the McDonald's theme song. I never asked why. I wouldn't be caught dead in a McDonald's, I should add.

"Many of my clients were musically inclined. There was

one very generous guy who wore a cowboy hat, a holster, a toy gun, and absolutely nothing else during our sessions; he used to leave them at my place together with a CD of "Home on the Range," which we listened to over and over. I now know every syllable of that annoying song. I'm not even going to mention the really kooky ones, but most of them were very appreciative, because my philosophy was essentially not to be judgmental and to collect the cash. Even Freddy reappeared. Why not, this way he could employ me only part time, on a piece-work basis, so to speak. No benefits, bing bang thank you man, he could have me and the Fefferbaums, too. I was a business, a thriving one, and that's how it went until four years ago when Dad died. My mom and dad had visited me once in New York. I had dreaded that visit. He had almost a sixth sense for things. I know that he sensed what was happening in my life, at least that I was gay. He never said a word but he knew, I could see it in his eyes; he seemed so sad, so cold.

"After they left, Dad never really spoke to me again, not one full sentence. I called many times. Mom was polite but vague, Dad basically would not talk. He died a year and a half later without one more real conversation with me. My sister called to tell me and I rushed home. Both Sally, who now lived in California with two kids, and I were shocked at how my mother had deteriorated. Dad must have been taking care of everything. She was disoriented, forgetful. In the next weeks we took her to a doctor and she was diagnosed with Alzheimer's. Sally couldn't come back to Akron but I could.

"For a few weeks I wrestled with the idea of moving back home, to take care of Mom. But how would I make a living? My particular skills might not be as widely in demand back home as they were in New York. And I was making big bucks. I had pretty much decided against it when Mom left the gas on one night and almost killed us all. That was it, I made arrangements and moved back. There were some moments, rare ones, when she was almost herself again, or maybe I imagined so. I spent almost three years there. Sally would come in two or three times a year to spell me. It was really hard. Luckily I met a number of kindred spirits in town, especially a dentist who helped generously with my finances. My mother was never so far gone that I could in all conscience put her in a nursing home. I fed her, I bathed her, I brushed her hair. What else could I do? I couldn't afford help.

"And then one morning, about a year ago, she didn't wake up. I came into her room with breakfast and she was gone. I didn't have to touch her, I knew immediately. She looked so peaceful, so serene, I was almost glad for her. I had to sell the house. Akron is not Fifth Avenue, but I prayed to St. Joseph and sure enough I found a buyer right away. Everybody knows that if you bury a statue of St. Joseph on the property it really speeds things up and I buried three of them. Sally and I split everything and I came back to New York."

Clarissa praises him. "That was a remarkable thing for you to do, especially after your parents had rejected you."

"Not my mother, she just obeyed my father but she never changed toward me. I owed her as good an end as I could provide. It wasn't easy, but I feel it was the best thing I ever did, best for me as well as best for her."

"Why did you let your father find out about your lifestyle? You could have been more careful. You must have known how he would react?" I ask. Why, indeed; maybe to hurt him, to stick it in his eye.

"I hid all the obvious things, none of my clients were allowed to call me while my parents were there. But he was too shrewd, things didn't make sense, the rent I paid, the clothes I had, it didn't compute with my lack of a job. He kept on probing, asking questions. Finally, I just clammed up, I put him off. I'm not a great liar. And then on the Friday before the weekend when they were leaving the doorman handed him my mail. God, how could I have forgotten? The gay paper, two gay magazines. I remember the moment he handed them to me, his eyes searching mine. He didn't know that I was a—whatever—a boy toy, but I'm sure he knew I was gay. And not another word about any of it, just that long silence, stilted sentences, complete dismissal. Thank God he couldn't know about the other, thank God for that. At least he didn't have to live through that."

Essie pipes in. "I don't know what to say, what to think. I'm not going to talk sweetie-sweetie to you, boy, I'm telling you like it is. You have to pray to the Lord to forgive the iniquity of your sin. And He will, He is mighty to forgive. I'll pray for you, we all will."

I am silent, the guy was a hooker. Who am I to judge, I certainly kept some female members of his trade busy in my time. And some of them were nice people, like he seems to be. But I want to know what he did after he returned to New York, did he go back to that? So I ask him. Before he can answer, Mendel interrupts. So he was listening all along. Mendel has become the defense attorney for us all it seems.

"Don't answer him, son," Mendel urges him. And to me, Mendel says, "And you shouldn't have asked such a question. What do you think he became, a brain surgeon? I don't care what he did to make money, to me it is of little importance. But what he did for his mother, that's the important thing and if there is a God in Heaven that's what He'll look at, that's what He'll count. When I was a boy in Gyor, I went to religious school, we learned many stories there, stories of rabbis, of heroes. And I remember the story of Rabbi Joshua; he was one of the great ones, he lived in Israel in ancient times. One night, this great man had a dream, and again the next night. In the dream he was told that in Heaven he would be sitting for eternity next to a man named Nanas, who was a butcher. Such a dream, a great rabbi and a butcher.

"So the rabbi wanted to find out why, he went and visited the butcher in his shop, the man was cutting the chickens and the meat. When the butcher saw the great rabbi, he was shocked. And when the rabbi asked him to tell him about his life, he didn't know what to say, he was a simple man. Finally he spoke about his work, his wife and children. The rabbi kept on pushing, what else, what else. 'Oh,' said the butcher, 'the only other thing is that I have both my parents still living, they're poor and weak so every day I stop by, I make them a meal, I bathe them, and clean their clothes and I sit with them a little before I go home.' 'Every day?' asked the rabbi. 'Every day,' said the butcher, 'they don't have anyone else, so I do it.' And the rabbi was very moved, he hugged the butcher and cried out, 'Blessed be God, Who has decided to grant me the privilege of spending eternity next to Nanas the butcher.' And so, young man, don't be scared. I think you will be welcomed in the Court, they'll celebrate when they see you. That's what I think."

Mendel's outburst troubles me. I put my mother in a nursing home, the finest one. I paid through the nose and I had to make huge contributions to it, too. She was slipping, her memory was going, what could I do? I wasn't happy about it, but I don't think it was wrong. I visited her as often as I could. What was I supposed to do, close my business, give up my social life? Maybe it worked in Gyor or in ancient Israel, maybe with Brett because what else did he have to do? Peddle his wares? A profitable hour or two in the sack with that dentist filling his cavity and then he could go back to being the perfect son. Sorry, I don't agree, I don't think the kid's a saint. Mendel is supersensitive, he feels he didn't do right by his own father so this moves him. There's more to life than that. I had a busy life, lots of responsibilities. I'm not going to let anyone make me feel guilty.

Here's Essie again, reciting her simple faith.

"He's right!" she exclaims, her voice excited. "Mendel is right. In our Bible it says 'fear your mother and your father,' fear them, and in the commandments it says 'honor them.' And you did both. And I believe that will wash away your sins. We're all sinners but you will be covered under the blood. I thank you, Lord, in the name of Jesus. Thank you, Lord."

Tears roll down her cheeks, if she could, if she still had the strength in her body, she would hug him, you can see it. What a nice lady, even if she's a little off. Must be in her eighties, nice to have that kind of faith.

After a few quiet minutes, Essie looks at each of us and then at Malakh.

"It's my turn now, isn't it? It's my turn. My memory isn't as good as it used to be, but I'll do my best. And if I forget anything big, you'll know it, won't you, and you'll remind me, right?"

Malakh agrees. I listen intently, I now have to admit that everybody is full of surprises, life is too mean and hard to be boring. It's just like my mother always said, each person is a complete little world of their own moving around in a big world. This old black lady could turn out to be a surprise, I'm listening, who knows, she could have been quite a number in her day. We all concentrate on Essie now as she begins her story.

"You all know my name by now—Essie Mae. I was born on a farm near Columbia in South Carolina eight-eighty years ago. Eight-eighty years, who would believe it? And I was still kicking, still moving around, still doing a little work until the accident. And I thank God for each day I had, they weren't all easy days but I thank Him for them. You're supposed to thank Him for even the tough days and I had plenty of them. And I'm thankful for my family, I was raised in a good family, hardworking, honest folks. Malakh, could I see my folks, my old house? Do you have a picture for me?"

And we all see a wooden house, ramshackle, weathered, an open porch, a pebbly path, and a couple of little girls moving about, busy.

"There I am!" exclaims Essie. "That's me in the yellow shorts. I'm holding Ida, the little one, and trying to clean that mud off of Beulah. Always messing herself up, Beulah; you wouldn't know it now but it was sure true then. If she fed the chickens, half the feed landed on her. And forget about feeding the hogs, more mud on her than on them. I was the oldest, I was in charge, I raised them with my momma. Momma, she was busy from morning to night, I don't know how she did it. Malakh, could I see my momma and my daddy? I'd love to see them again. My daddy was still around until I was twelve, then he was killed in an accident, crushed. He tried hard to raise us right but he had no business taking that job at the mill and then working the farm. He was tired and that's what got him, crushed like that, he didn't see it coming. I remember that afternoon, my momma screaming, so were the girls. But not me, I cried all right but no screaming. All the screaming was out of me by then; no use screaming, it don't change a thing. Not me, even then I turned my eyes to the Lord, little Miss-Grin-and-Bear-It, Beulah used to call me, and that's the truth, that was me. Please, Malakh, let me see my momma and my daddy."

And we all see them, a tired-looking big woman with a kind face, the kindness shining out of her eyes, the father a strong, grizzled-looking man. Essie looks a lot like him, you can see the resemblance. Next to me, she is silent, fixated on the images. No tears, no sighs, just silence. After a long while, she turns to Malakh.

"Thank you," she says, "thank you so much," her voice soft and velvety.

"And James," she adds, "could I see my James? I knew him from church since I can remember, I never guessed he had his eye on me. He didn't show it, I was sure surprised," her face smiling with the pleasure of the memory. "Could I see him when he came courting? He was a fine-looking man, him and those flowers he brought, posies he said, picked from his field."

A young black man, sturdy and sure of himself, and a very young Essie emerge before our eyes, walking down a country road, holding hands. He carefully helps her over the uneven, unpaved road. An ordinary scene, the two stealing glances at each other, in no hurry as they amble along. And yet, it's clear as day that they're together, in love. Every little movement, every little quick smile betrays it. You can't help but smile at the sight, that's what young couples look like, they think they've discovered something unique, that they've invented love.

"We waited until I was seventeen, James was twenty. I was still needed at home, until Beulah could handle things. And then I moved into James's place and we were married. It wasn't fancy, but those were the best years. I had my two boys, my Willy and my Charlie, and we were okay. Then James decided we had to go up North, most everyone was doing it and why should we be different? Factories were opening up, there were jobs in New York, you didn't have to haul your water, there were doctors up North, toilets in the house. Our cousins moved on up, they encouraged us to come up, too. And we did, we brought Momma and the girls with us and we moved to Brooklyn and we left the farm behind. We just walked on out, never looked back. And we also left the meanness, the separate seats, the water fountains you couldn't drink from, good riddance to all of that. We were moving on up."

Essie smiles somewhat wistfully.

"Not that life in Brooklyn was easy; James got a job driving a truck and I began to clean houses. And in those days, there was so much hard labor. Three nights a week I did laundry in a big apartment house in New York. In those years you had to go down to the basement, hand wash the clothes, and then string them up on a line and pull that line through a steam room to dry, twice sometimes. Thank the Lord, I was strong, that farm work had made me strong, but I had to do all that after a day's cleaning and it was hard.

"Life was okay, we had enough. Momma watched my boys; they were growing up and we didn't want them to mix it up with those street kids. They get big enough, they do whatever they're big enough to do and no way that was going to be true for our boys. There were gang fights, knives, some-times even shooting on the streets, and I had to work, so did James. Momma had trouble with Willy, especially, he was already sixteen, but James put the fear of God into that boy and we were managing. In the summer, James would take Willy with him when he had a trucking job—to keep him busy, to teach him. He meant it for the best, he would do anything for his boys."

Here Essie stops, her expression a chilling mixture of sadness and restraint. Oh, no, I think, not the boy, not her kid. Not after all that, I hope not. But something must have happened. We wait, but Essie says nothing more, she obviously has run out of steam.

After some time, Malakh speaks, his voice sympathetic, his cadence slow and gentle.

"It was the morning of July seventh, nineteen forty-eight. Father and son were together in the truck, heading for Poughkeepsie with a load of grocery supplies. It was raining, the road was slick. It was nobody's fault, an accident. They both died instantly. The state troopers were sure that neither one suffered, they died on impact. They assured you of that, Essie, they told you that your boy didn't suffer. You remember that, don't you?"

No reply. Essie looks at each one of us, her eyes are teary and her jaw clenched tight. No sound emerges, you could hear a pin drop.

Malakh tries to help. "You took them back home, down South, and you buried them in the family plot. You brought them back home, Essie."

"It didn't matter where I buried them, once you're gone, what difference does it make? Momma wanted them there, so I did it; she passed on and joined them there about a year later. It was Charlie and me, that's all that was left; he was fifteen, I was in my late thirties. But I couldn't live in that old apartment any more, I couldn't stand it. We moved to a place on Bergen Street and I thank the Lord for that, I thank Him for that move. Three doors down was the Holy Zion House of Prayer and that became my salvation, and Charlie's. That's where I made my decision for the Lord, that's where I learned to turn everything over to Him, to His Will. And if I hadn't, I don't know what would have happened to us, we would have been blown away like the dust of the earth. But I gave it over to Him and He gave me the strength I needed, He never failed me, He took me through.

"Charlie, too, he's a deacon in his church, three children, he works for the city, he has a nice house, he makes me proud. Most Sundays, he picks me up and we have lunch together. He's a good man. And it's all from the Lord, thank you, Jesus, I thank Him for each day I had. But Charlie has his burdens, too; his boy is in trouble now, he fell in with some bad boys. I've been praying for him. I'd like to have a chance to ask the Lord for help with him. I don't want no drugs in my family, I need the help of the Lord here. Will I have a chance to plead for my boy? When can I do it?"

Malakh assures her, "No problem. You can do it when
you stand before the Court. But there is another scene I
must bring into view for you, we have to talk about it. After
James and Willy died, things were tough at home. Not
enough money was coming in. Charlie needed you but you
had to work, you needed to keep your day job and your
laundering work at night. During the days, five and a half
days a week, you cleaned for the Perry family on Fifth
Avenue, you worked for them for over thirty years. They
were decent people; you loved their little girl, Patsy, you
helped bring her up."

"Yes," agrees Essie, "I raised her. Mrs. Perry was a big-
time lawyer and Mr. Perry traveled a lot for business. I raised
Patsy, I loved her like my own. She was a good child. I'd
take her to the park when she was little and she'd obey,
never run away, never talk back. Not like her mother. Now
that woman was a mean woman, she was mean and she
would make me angry, at the last minute make me stay late,
no warning, over and over again, to watch Patsy. She knew
I had Charlie at home, she knew he needed watching, too.
But she knew I needed the job, she was a selfish woman;
sometimes I wouldn't get home 'til after midnight. I had to
put bread on the table, pay the rent."

"Nothing is forgotten, not here. Neither her mean spirit
nor your hard labor is forgotten. But let me show you something, Essie, as a reminder."

And what appears is a small collection of jewelry, strands of pearls, some rings, and a pair of small diamond earrings. They are set out, on display, and as each piece appears Essie flinches.

"That was before I turned to the Lord, before I let Him into my life. It was a terrible time, my momma had just died, I needed money to take her down South and bury her. And who would watch Charlie? I needed to pay for my neighbor to make him supper, to make sure he did his homework. You know, that's when the devil pays you a visit—when you're down, when you're scared. Mrs. Perry's mother died and left some jewelry; they brought it home in a bag, a paper bag, and left it in a drawer in the den. And it sat there for months, more than a year. Nobody cared, maybe they forgot about it. I needed over a thousand dollars. That was a lot of money in those days, I was desperate.

"My next door neighbor told me she couldn't take care of Charlie anymore unless I paid, she needed money herself. What could I do? We were behind on the rent. I kept on thinking of those earrings. How could they forget about them? So I took them, one night when Mrs. Perry ordered me to stay late, her husband was away and she wanted to play cards with some friends. Charlie was alone. I wondered what he would eat for supper. I was angry, Lord knows. That night I took the earrings and I pawned them a week later. It fixed a lot of problems. Months went by, years went by, and nobody knew nothing, nobody ever asked about them. That bag is probably still sitting there.

"I would polish that table every two weeks and nobody ever touched that bag again. I know it was wrong, I knew it then. But I was desperate, what could I do? I could never redeem those earrings, the Lord knows I never had enough money to do that. Can you imagine having enough so that you can just forget about diamonds? That's rich, no fooling around rich. But you're right to remind me, 'cause I stole and it was wrong. I never did it again, never would, but I am guilty, I did that." Essie hangs her head.

"I'll trust in His mercy. I'm no saint and I did wrong. But I'm not ashamed to stand before Him, I'll face His judgment. Are you finished, any more of the devil's work you have to accuse me of? What else have I done? I'm sure you'll find other things, I wasn't no saint, the Lord knows I wasn't. I'll trust in His mercy." She turns away from Malakh, her expression firm, her attitude proud. "If there's nothing else, I'm finished, I'll wait for my God."

"Just one more thing," says Malakh, as he looks warily at Mendel. "I don't mean to make too much of it but there is one more item we should discuss. When you were doing that laundry work, that heavy labor, there was a gentleman who helped you. He helped you pull those rope lines through the steam room, remember? He was a real friend to you, here he is."

And up comes the image of a man, an older white man, gray-haired and pale, dressed in an undershirt and jeans. He's pulling on the lines with Essie and they're laughing at something he's saying, he's pointing to some very large boxer shorts hanging on the line. Essie covers her eyes with one hand, she wipes away tears of laughter. "Stop, Mac, stop," she pleads, "you and your naughty mouth. Anyone hears us they'll fire me and then what'll I do?"

"Okay, I'll be good," he replies. "I wouldn't want you to lose this great job; hell, you'd miss being down here, flirting with me."

"Flirting? Flirting? How could you say that, Mac? Let me tell you, if I was flirting, you'd know it, you'd be on your knees. Flirting? No way and you know it." She seems genuinely horrified. Mac looks at her intently, there's a lot going on inside him, you can feel it. They're both sweaty and tired-looking, he's wiping the sweat off his forehead with his arm but he still leans in and helps her pull that line.

"I was just kidding," he says, "don't be angry."

He grabs her left hand and pats it, you can see that he wants to do more but he settles for the pat.

"I could never be angry at you, Mac, never. You are so kind. I don't know if I'd be able to keep this no account job if it wasn't for your help, and I know you're plenty tired after a day's work. I was just fooling with you, don't feel bad."

My God, I think, that must have been in the 1950s, he's white, she's black, he's old, she's young. Unusual.

Next to me, Essie's voice is silken, soft.

"I'm so happy to see him again, that good man. He helped me when I was real low. I believe the good Lord sent Mac to me because I cried out to Him. I was tired, so lonely, and I think Mac was, too. He was much older, all alone. And I wasn't flirting with him. I never was much for flirting— didn't have to be, they came after me. Mac did, too, and I'm not ashamed. I was a widow. Neither of us was married and if he had been a black man, I would have married him. But back then it wasn't possible. Mac wanted to but I couldn't do it to Charlie, I couldn't do it to my boy. We would have been like fish out of water, no way I would do that to Charlie. So I slept with that old man, is that what you're after, Malakh? I did that, that was no sin, I don't think so. For almost five years he comforted me and no living soul ever knew about it. Right there, in the basement of that building where he was the super.

"Yessir, sometimes he'd have a vase of flowers; he knew I loved flowers. After a while he went and painted flowers all over the walls of his room, he did it himself. He told me they were for me, so I'd always have flowers when I was with him. I sure loved him and when he died suddenly—it was his heart—I went to his funeral. Everybody stared at me but I went, I needed to say goodbye. They could stare 'til

Kingdom Come but I loved that good man. I'm happy to see him again now, that good face, those big strong hands. God rest his soul. All these memories, they're heavy, a heavy burden. Only the Lord can help you carry them, you have to lean on His shoulder, His rod and His staff they will comfort you. Let me rest now, Malakh. If you're finished, so am I."

Enough silence follows so that it is clear that Essie's interrogation is over. I realize, oh, no, it's my turn, nobody left but me. Fasten your seat belts, I think, wait until this crowd gets a load of my life. The only one who probably tops me is Brett, our friendly hooker, and even he seems to have redeeming characteristics. I'm not meeting Malakh's gaze. I'll keep my eyes down, buy some time. Essie swiped a pair of earrings and she's being reminded of it; how is the Court going to react to some of my business deals, perfectly legal but a little inventive. And all my fooling around, God alone knows how many women. Let's see, thirty-seven years of marriage, at least two or three new faces a year, there won't be time for Malakh to go into all that, he's going to have to pick and choose. And until the accident I never really suffered that much in my life; Clarissa and Essie, and certainly Mendel, struggled a lot, that has to count to their credit. I've got to try to follow Brett into Court, after him maybe they'll be less judgmental. After all, nobody ever paid me for sex, quite the contrary; I was the disbursing agent, I must have shelled out hundreds of thousands over the years. You want to play, you've got to pay. So what's so terrible, I was always kind to the ladies, always generous. Of course it was adultery but not many of the girls were married, I don't think it's so terrible if the girls are single.

I'm going to look like shit to the Court if I'm in this batch, even Brett has that good deed with his mother, what do I have? My charities, maybe they will help. I gave the museum that room in the Contemporary Wing. Never liked that art, scrawls and scribbles that contemporary crap, but they put my name up. And after my surgery I went on the board at the hospital; they save your ass, you feel like you've got to pay. I don't know how much that makes up for. I also endowed Bobby's school, had to, he was a lousy student and I needed to keep them happy. And how about that college library I refurbished? God alone knows if Bobby would have gotten in without that hundred grand. What I didn't do for that kid while he repeatedly spit in my eye, told me I was trying to smother him, I should lay off. He'd be sucking the farts out of seat covers right now if I hadn't smoothed his way. Instead he's living in a grand home in Greenwich with that big bargain he married. I don't think I ever heard a thank you out of him, it was all coming to him, our little prince.

My reverie is interrupted.

"Irving," invites Malakh, "how about a word or two

from you? We've got to move things along here, souls are waiting for me."

I've got an idea.

"Malakh," I say, "I'm not much for reviewing the past, I don't really believe in it. I always lived for the present and for the future. Why don't we have a look at the present down on earth, my wife, my son, my business? Looking back is not always advisable—remember Lot's wife in the Bible? Didn't she turn to salt when she looked back at Sodom? Let's start from the present."

"Forget it," counters Malakh, "knock it off. Either you recite your story or I will and if I do it, you might be surprised at how much is remembered. Names, addresses, phone numbers, the works. So what's your preference, you doing it or me?"

Well, that didn't work. I've got a grumpy angel on my hands. It was worth a try, if you don't ask, you don't get. "Okay, I hear you, you're the boss. But you shouldn't hold it against me that I knew lots of people and that I grew close to many of them. I was a man of many interests, of many parts. Don't judge me harshly."

"I don't judge you at all, the High Court will do that. Why not stop horsing around and start talking? There's been a shooting in Spanish Harlem; young kids come up, they're always so scared. More souls coming up every hour. No rest for the weary, that's Archangel Uriel's favorite saying and it's God's honest truth. So get a move on, please, I want you to talk it out. You'll feel a lot better."

Wrong, is he wrong. Dredging up all the shit is not going to make me feel better. Oh, look, he's bringing up my parent's apartment on Ocean Avenue, second floor back. Look at the step down to the living room, nice room, my mother kept it so clean. There are the plastic covers for the sofas, I remember how warm it got to sit on them; you could move around on them and produce a sound like a fart. Those covers came off only on state occasions and on the big holidays. And there's my canary, Wilbur. I loved that dirty little bird, feathers floating around and that endless noise. Cruel, I suppose, to lock up a bird, but I loved it. I used to whistle to it while it looked at me quizzically, cocking its head and staring at me.

Good old Brooklyn, what a great place to grow up that was. Nobody we knew had an extra dime, but who knew? I didn't feel poor but nobody had to lecture me on not wasting money, the lessons were all around. My father dragged himself to work in the garment district in Manhattan; imagine his job as a tailor and presser. Nobody had air-conditioning in those years. The summers must have been hell for him and then he had to take the subway back and forth. Sometimes he would come home looking pale and exhausted, my mother would worry; *such heat*, she would mutter to herself over and over. "Poor man," she would say as we waited supper for him. My God, this Malakh must be able to read my mind, there's my father now; he used to look like an old man to me but now I see he was probably in his late forties when we lived there. And there's my mother, nobody wears an apron like that anymore, a frilly apron like that. I'm not even sure anybody cooks anymore, God knows Jane doesn't.

"Jake, it's after seven," my mother complains. "What happened, did that murderer make you stay late in this heat again? That killer. For a dollar extra, he'd kill you, he should rot in hell."

"It's okay, I'm okay. I had to stay, we had to finish a shipment for Gimbel's, what could I do?"

"What can I get you, a little nosh, some crackers, some tomato juice?"

"No thanks, I've got to take a shower first, I couldn't eat anything until I cool off. Trying to eat now would be like trying to feed a corpse, I'm half dead from this heat. Give me fifteen minutes, no more."

"My God, how they loved each other," I say to the others. "He never got up from the table without thanking her, such a nice meal, thank you, dear. Little courtesies were never forgotten, no matter what and I never heard them fight. Argue, yes, but not fight, no raised voices. Not in front of me anyway, and no matter how rough things got, my father would shrug his shoulders and philosophize. 'If you live long enough,' he would say, 'you have to live through everything.' That's how he greeted each new outrage that life threw his way. He had this Yiddish expression, *azoi gaytes*—that's how it goes,—he would say, his hands uplifted in a gesture of resignation.

"When his heart condition was diagnosed, he took the same attitude. 'You can't live forever, thank God,' he would say, 'and who would want to?' Well, he didn't have to worry about living forever, he died when he was fifty-two on the steps of the subway. And that ended my college education. I was the only child and there was no money, I never even gave it much thought. That's how it goes, I said to myself."

Gee, I'm beginning to enjoy this, it's fun to talk about yourself and these people have to listen, they can't drift away. Not only that, but they'll probably be polite, too. Not bad.

Malakh apparently thinks I've run out of material so he produces one of his slide shows. There's Jane, boy, was she cute, I don't think she was more than eighteen, nineteen when we met. The boss's daughter. I thought her father was so rich; he ran the textile company my father had worked for and I now slaved at. Sometimes I would deliver something from the business to their home on Central Park West. Doormen and elevator men in uniform, first time I ever was in such a building. On one of those visits, she came to the door; her hair was dark and pulled into a ponytail and I remember she was wearing a red dress. Big brown eyes and what a smile. And I was shlepping a big parcel, sweating, not too cheerful, and when I saw her I went into shock. My throat went dry, I could hardly speak. I croaked out my name and handed her the package, it was for her. She thanked me, asked me if I wanted some cold water. Sure, I wanted that water and that's not all I wanted.

I resume my monologue. "That's how I met Jane, my wife," I point out to the folks. "We've been married just under forty years. Her parents were not too thrilled; her mother pointed out that I had nothing, nothing at all and that Jane was a rich girl. They fought hard against it but they lost the battle."

"You were so handsome, that's why," comments Clarissa. "Look at that lock of hair falling into your face, and what a great face. You look something like Frank."

"You were handsome." adds Brett. "What a waste that you were straight."

"Enough already with how handsome." chimes in Mendel. "Handsome is as handsome does, no? Let the man finish so we can get down to brass tacks here. So talk."

"Malakh, I'd like to see my wedding, it was great. At the Essex House on Central Park South, more than two hundred people, thirty or forty from our side, the rest from theirs. Listen, they were paying, they called the shots."

And Malakh brings up the scene, the ballroom, Mom—

how happy and proud she looked. All dressed up—wearing the gold necklace Dad had bought her just about a year before he died, her hair done in that funny artificial-looking way they used to wear it—she looks beautiful to me. Her demeanor guarded, she obviously felt ill at ease in that ballroom, too grand for her. I remember her whispering to me in awe. 'These people must be stuffed with money like you'd stuff a goose,' she said, the food, the music, the jewelry.

Clarissa asks, "Were they really so rich, as rich as you thought?"

Clever woman.

"No," I answer honestly, "not really. But to me then they sure seemed to be. Who knows what rich means? Sometimes I think that rich is twice whatever you happen to have. It's a moving target. Still, it was quite a wedding."

And we see Jane, in her gown and veil, and me, look how skinny I was, in my rented tails. The wedding canopy covered with flowers, and the Jewish music, each of us lifted up on a chair, laughing and happy. Not a bad beginning to our life together. And it was a good life together, plenty of ups and downs, a few skirmishes, one or two really bad moments. All the compromises we each had to make, all the little annoyances we each had to swallow; some people might call it hard labor but that's what makes for a good marriage. I'm sure Jane was faithful to me and I know I was always loyal to her in the deepest sense of the word.

All my fooling around never really changed the way I felt
about her, I believe that. I took over her family's business,
built it up, and before I sold it there were years of temptations, all those models we used to show our seasonal lines,
wave after wave of them, what was I supposed to do? A man
is different from a woman; he should be judged differently,
even up here.

There's a view of Bobby as a newborn, I'm standing in
the hospital corridor looking through the glass at him. Mom
is next to me, my in-laws, too. They're arguing gently, ever
so gently, about the baby's name. Mom wants Jacob after
my Dad, they want Robert for my father-in-law's father.
They tell her it's the mother's right to name the first child;
not when there is someone in the family who hasn't yet been
named for, she replies. It's hard for Mom, she still pins
Dad's death on overwork by Jane's father, plenty of con-
cealed resentment there.

"Hey, a baby has two names, a first one and a middle
one, we can use them both," I plead.

"A middle name is nothing," my mother forges on, "a
middle name is not right for a father."

"Jane will decide," I say, "let her decide, talk to her."
Jesus, you can't have a minute's peace, not even when you
look at your newborn kid. "There'll be other kids, probably,
let's not fight over a name."

My mother knows she's going to lose this one, you can

see it in her face. But in my family, defeat did not bring silence.

"Look what he did for you," she says, "what a father he was. He died going to work, he was so determined that you should finish college, he dragged himself to work with that heart condition. For us he did it, for you."

This is ostensibly directed at me but she is gunning for my father-in-law, going for his jugular. He doesn't flinch.

"Let Jane decide, she's the mother. Who are we to push, leave it to her," he suggests.

He knows he's already won, why should he lose his temper?

As that picture fades, the pain of that moment still pierces me.

"There were no other kids," I say to the folks around me, "so my Dad never did get named for. I don't think my mother ever forgave me. I'll never forget her look at the bris, at the circumcision, when Bobby was officially named. What could I do, I worked for them. Jane wanted her grandfather's name, what could I do? Why does everything in a family have to be so difficult? Was that my fault, too? You can't make everybody happy, and at that moment I stopping trying. Two days after the bris was my first infidelity. I'm not justifying it, but I needed a little vacation from the family, a little time-out. And Blythe was available and very experienced.

"To her it was one more little incident on the way to a successful modeling career; to me it was an icebreaker; that's not the right word, it was a firecracker. Delightful sex and no strings attached, not much conversation and, surprisingly, no guilt. Not even a moment of guilt. That's when I learned the particular therapeutic value of oral sex; it feels good and the woman can't speak to you while she's performing it. It's a double bubble, perfection. And since then I never stopped. Sometimes I paid in cash, sometimes in soothing words, sometimes in advice and counsel. I always tried to be kind and thoughtful; sometimes I actually think that I did a lot more good than harm. I subsidized at least two college educations, I helped some of the ladies with career decisions, I paid for at least one psychiatrist, I did some good deeds. You could even say that it was a positive experience, sometimes a mitzvah."

I stop and wait to gauge the reaction. Mendel snorts. Clarissa throws a sarcastic look at me.

"In that case," she says, "you should have done even more of it. All those good deeds of yours would have piled up and assured you of Seventh Heaven."

Brett seems to agree with me. "When done in a spirit of openness and kindness, sex can be a good deed. I certainly feel that way about my career. I've done a lot more good than bad. When my clients would finish they would glow with pleasure, there was more bounce to their steps, I could see what a positive effect I had on them. I think, in a somewhat different way, you and I changed the world just a little for the better."

I look at Essie. What is she going to say, have I convinced her? She looks at me intently, she looks like she feels sorry for me.

"You joking, boy, are you joking? Lord have mercy, I can't believe you're talking that way up here on the road to judgment. I'm not fooling with you, boy, you did wrong. You broke the commandment and you did whatever you were big enough to do. You're gonna pay for that unless you repent. This is no time for foolishness."

Too bad, I had the rest of them softening. I glance at Malakh, he's got a twinkle in his eye. "Let's see one of your good deeds in action, Irving. Maybe it'll prove your point. Lean back and let's have a look."

Oh, no, not that room at the Waldorf, not Vera, oh, shit. We see Vera come in; she is a brassy, big, and loud blonde in her forties. I greet her in my little red bikini underpants, what a sight.

Clarissa screams out, "Vera! That's Vera Dorsey! I hated her, she was my biggest competition as a personal shopper, she stole two of my best accounts. A witch, a tricky witch. And that so-called Hermes bag she's carrying, a copy from Hong Kong. The real Hermes never made a color like that. Puce—more like puke. It's a fake and she was a fake. What's she doing in your hotel room?"

They can all see I'm in my underpants—what am I supposed to reply?

"She is Jane's personal shopper, she directs all her clothing purchases."

This is what I say as we all watch Vera take off all of her clothes rather hastily.

"Irv," she says as she disrobes, "we have to make it quick. I've got a 4:30 appointment with two Saudi women who drop big bucks. The thought of my commission alone is making me excited but the sight of you in those shorts is driving me over the brink. Take them off and get on your back."

This as she pulls off her own floral undies.

"Wait!" I yell to Malakh. "You never showed any sex act before, it isn't fair."

"Quiet down." he replies. "There's no way to depict your life without depicting the sex act. You spent at least a quarter of your waking hours either in the act or working on it."

"What about Brett, didn't he make his living waving his ass in front of every man of means he ever met, why did he escape your slide show? It isn't fair."

"Believe it or not, Brett spent only a tenth of his waking time at it, an hour here or there, ten or twelve times a week. And he was not married; there was no adultery. He did it to make a living, it was really his only outstanding talent. With you, either you were in bed or wining and dining them, plotting and planning, hiring and firing for that purpose. It was the center of your life and you now claim it was done for reasons of kindness. Well, let's have a look."

And we all see me strip and lie down, Vera climbing on top of me. We actually make an attractive picture, let them look, who cares?

"Talk to me," says Vera, "make me want it, baby."

I forgot, this is a little embarrassing, the way Vera needed to be aroused. I'm lying there quite ready and I begin my litany.

"I'm planning on buying Jane that Chanel suit you showed her, probably this week. The fifty-eight hundred dollar one with the ribbons."

"Oh, yes." says Vera as she mounts me, "but what about the navy blue one with the white piping? She loved the piping. I loved it, too."

This as she slowly moves up and down on top of me.

"That one, too, if you think so. Okay, how much is it?"

"It's only thirty-seven hundred, it's on presale. She must have it, oh, yes, oh, you feel so good."

"And jewelry, Jane mentioned earrings by de Grisogono, ruby ones."

"Yes, yes, ruby drop earrings, earrings to die for, or even better, to live for, I can get a discount on them, I love rubies."

She's pumping away now, harder.

I'm losing my breath, I'm gasping, but I continue.

"And the sable!" I yell, "The sable coat, oh, the golden sable, oh, the fluffy sable! You'll negotiate, won't you, you'll get me a discount? She loved the sable."

Now Vera is gasping, too; her face is red.

"I'm so close," she announces. "More, give me more, I need more!"

"A sable hat," I add, "to complete the look. You can include a hat."

"A hat," she repeats, "a hat, yes, oh, yes, one more purchase, just one more and I'm over the top. Don't stop, don't stop now," she pleads.

"A muff, a sable muff," I pant, "a big fluffy muff."

"Yes!" Vera screams, "yes, yes, yes."

And we both shake in unison, our passion consummated, sweating and heaving. After a moment or two, Vera leans over to the night table, grabs a pad and pen, and makes notes.

"The Chanels," she recalls, "that incredible pair of earrings," she pants, "and the sables. Oh, the coat I can get for under a hundred thousand, the hat I'll get for seven or eight thou, the muff they'll have to make to order—let's say ten. I'll make a hidden pocket in it. Jane will love it, what a lucky lady she is."

And she kisses me perkily on my nose as the vision begins to fade.

"You see," I declare to Malakh and the others. "Look how happy I made that poor woman, a hardworking woman, the sole support of her family. There is a good deed in there somewhere, I believe that. I feel vindicated."

"God, I wish you were gay," says Brett. "Nobody ever paid me that way. I had to earn mine a few hundred at a time; great men's bodies are a dime a dozen, it's really not fair. She must have made five percent or more in commissions, a fortune."

"I can't believe that you spent all that money through Vera, a woman of no real taste at all. Terminally ordinary taste. She wouldn't have known a good sable from a stone marten. What a waste," laments Clarissa.

"Lord have mercy," says Essie, "people are hungry, don't have a decent bathroom and hot water and some of these women spending a hundred thousand dollars for a coat. Lord, I'm glad I didn't know that while I was living, I'm sure glad of that."

"This is some world, " says Mendel, "this is a rotten world. This you defend, Irving, this is your good deed, not charity, not kindness but this, you and that piece of *drek*, of shit, and you think you did a mitzvah? What a world."

I look at Malakh, who I notice is staring directly at me.

"More?" he inquires, "Would you like to see Marla or Julie or Betty or Dina? Shall I continue? Or should I mention that eighteen-year-old from Utah, another good deed?

Or the so-called nineteen-year-old from the Bronx? When you found out she was still in high school you paid through the nose. Also a wonderful deed? And your occasional forays along Tenth Avenue, near the tunnel. Remember those kind moments? You were a saint. Saint Irving. They should name a street for you. If you were a Catholic, maybe they'd canonize you; they could build a shrine in your honor and desperate women could come there to offer their prayers."

"It's easy to make fun of me. That's a cheap shot, Malakh, you didn't speak to anybody else here in that way. Maybe you're jealous, maybe underneath all that holiness and light you're just plain jealous. Most of the women I was with would say nice things about me, they would have pleasant memories of me, I always showered before sex, slapped on a little cologne. Always considerate and always generous, money was no object. You're an angel, you never had sex, what do you know, how can you judge me?"

"I'll tell you how, my friend. Remember a lady named Madeleine, a secretary you hired maybe twenty years ago? Remember she had a sick mother whom she lived with in Queens? For you it was a little escapade, for her it was more that that. Does that ring a bell with you?"

"Sure," I reply. "She was a nut. That's not fair, how could I have known that she was a crackpot? It's my fault that after a few little encounters with me she began to stalk me? I paid for her psychiatrist, didn't I? Two hundred dollars a session, twice a week, for years. She tried to kill herself and that's also my fault? Unfair, you're being unfair. I'd like to change angels. Could I have another angel? I'm not your cup of tea, fine, I feel the same way. I'd like to start over with one of your colleagues."

"Forget it," says Malakh. "Life is unfair, so is the afterlife. You don't like me, too bad, you're stuck with me. Try not pulling the wool over my eyes. I'm thousands of years old, I've heard it all. But you're beginning to piss me off, so calm down. I look at your life—you married for what you thought was money, you parlayed the family business into quite a little empire, you raised a son who couldn't fight his way out of a paper bag, and you cheated on your wife on at least a weekly basis for the last thirty-something years. These were your achievements. Are there any good deeds you would like to mention before we move on?"

My luck, I've got myself a mean-spirited putz of an angel, but what can I do, I've got to make the best of it.

"Give me a minute," I say out loud, "let me think."

I don't imagine that my charitable contributions will move him but it's hard to think under this pressure. I must have done some things out of simple kindness, I've got to dredge them up. I look at him, I wilt under his gaze. I'm beginning to tremble here a little, I'm going to look like a bum to the High Court, I'm in deep shit.

Amazingly, Malakh himself comes to the rescue. He

definitely can read our minds, I'm sure of it now. He brings up a picture, I recognize the boy immediately. It's Bobby's old friend Danny, his classmate in high school. A good kid, a good influence on Bobby, Jane and I always liked him. Oh, right, I did that kid a good turn.

"Yes," I say out loud, "thanks, Malakh. Yes, I helped that boy. His mother and father divorced, she remarried and moved to Omaha, and then his Dad went broke. The kid had to get a scholarship for college and he couldn't swing it; there wasn't enough money for him to pay his expenses, he dropped out. I called his father, I volunteered to pay the kid's tuition and dorm room, and no one knew, not even the kid himself. I did that for the three remaining years of college. Yes, I'm proud of that, I had forgotten about it. I had to drop out of school when my Dad died, I knew what that felt like, I didn't want Danny to go through that. He's a lawyer now, he's doing well."

What a relief, I've got something in the credit column; I don't know if it's enough.

Malakh does it again. Another picture, this time of a little girl but I don't recognize her. Solemn faced, two long brown braids, maybe she's five or six years old. Who is she?

"Ronit Shternberg," Malakh says, as if in answer to my silent question. "Remember her?"

But I don't, I don't know who she is.

"Do you remember getting a telephone call from your

cousin in Israel about a little girl with a rare form of cancer who needed to be taken to Seattle for treatment? An experimental treatment costing a hundred fifteen thousand dollars. This was about twenty years ago. You remember?"

"Yes, sure. I rounded up the money, called a few friends. I gave the first twenty-five thousand and then the last seventy-five hundred to top it off. Yes. What happened to her? I lost track."

"They saved her, Irving, you helped save her. She got married last year, she lives in Jerusalem. I'll show you."

And we all see a beautiful young woman standing under a wedding canopy with a young man, he stomps on a glass and joyous music trumpets out, everyone shouts Mazel Tov. What a sight. That must be Ronit, it looks like I did something right. And I had forgotten all about it.

"Malakh, I apologize. Thanks for reminding me, I appreciate it."

"A good deed feels wonderful," he replies. "Even all these years later. Remember the old saying, if you save one life it's as if you saved the whole world. Everything is remembered here, there is no forgetting here, and that was a good deed, something that will accompany you to the judgment."

All is not lost, I'm still in the running. After all that living, all that tumult, that's what it seems to be boiling down to, two good deeds, not that great a record for a lifetime, I guess. But maybe I can still worm my way through. I still think I did some good with some of those women, I'm not giving up that argument just yet. I have to admit that Malakh has surprised me, he obviously doesn't really dislike me, he just likes to provoke me. Sorry I said that thing about changing angels, he didn't deserve that.

"Can you think of anything else, Irv? Come on, try."

But I cannot, the museums, the hospital, the schools, all that charity was self-serving. If I bring it up, he'll yell at me, he seems to know everything. So what's the use?

"Let me help you," he says. "You remember when you took over Hadson's, the candy company, more then twenty years ago. You remember that you discovered that the CFO had 'borrowed'—stolen really—eighteen thousand dollars. Remember how angry you were. You called him in to fire him and you were right to do so, nobody could argue. Dennis was his name, he broke down in your office."

"Yes, I remember. That was long ago. The man had worked for the company for almost thirty years; it was unbelievable, and all he took was eighteen thousand dollars. Why risk everything for that? It didn't make sense. He admitted he had a drinking problem, he claimed he had been drinking heavily only since his wife died. And that had led to gambling; he owed money to the wrong guys. I knew I had to fire him, you can't have a dishonest CFO. He couldn't repay the money, I should have reported him, had him sent to jail."

"But you didn't, did you? Why?"

"Well, I don't know for sure. He looked desperate, maybe I was afraid he'd kill himself. It was only eighteen grand, I didn't want to ruin his life over it. I don't know if I was right, to tell you the truth; he looked something like my father, I swear he did. I couldn't take the expression on his face, he reminded me of my Dad, that resigned look, used to suffering. So I swallowed it, I had bought the company, it was my money. I let him resign, why embarrass the guy, I let it go. Not the smartest business decision, maybe, but it made me feel good. He looked just like my Dad."

"Up here we have a saying," says Malakh. "He who shames another person in public, it's as though he killed him. The proof of that is that you can see the blood rushing up to his face when he is shamed. That's an important principle at the High Court."

"I saved him from that," I point out. I understand, Malakh is trying to help me again. "Later I thought I may have been a shmuck to do it but somehow I found myself forgiving him."

"You had mercy on him, that's what you had, be proud of it," interjects Essie. "You'll be blessed for it, you'll see."

"I agree," says Brett. "I don't know whether I would have been as understanding. That's a lot of money to me."

"You may not realize it," adds Malakh, "but that moment was one of the high points of your life, the way we measure things up here. And you didn't even understand it for what it was. You know, there are some people who earn eternal life in just a few seconds. You behaved well, I'm recording it in the book of your life, remember to bring it up at the Court."

But Malakh changes the subject.

"There's something else we need to discuss, something you have to clarify: your relationship with Jane. You need to understand it better. You were married for almost forty years. Didn't she ever get wind of your affairs, didn't she ever suspect anything? All those evening meetings, those business trips, never a peep out of her? Come on, she's no dope. What was going on?"

"I've thought hard about that for years now. Maybe she didn't care, maybe she was content with the setup, I don't know. I showered her with gifts, every luxury, maybe that satisfied her. She was always busy, keeping our two homes going, raising Bobby, attending her Hadassah meetings. She even went each year without me to Hadassah conventions all over the country. She was a busy woman. Hell, it worked, our marriage worked, don't fix it if it's not broken, that's what they say. And I loved her. Cheating has nothing to do with that, you can still love your wife—what does one thing have to do with another? To me, sex is a little friction, most of the pleasure comes from the hunt, from the conquest. She knew I loved her and that was obviously enough for her. Why probe, Malakh, why raise the issue?"

"Adultery, remember, we're talking about adultery here, one of the top ten, so to speak. Not one or two little slippages, but scores over the years. And all that money you spent on the ladies. Half of that money was your wife's; she was unwittingly paying for half of your fun. This is not the locker room at your club, this is your one and only afterlife. Get serious, will you; stop defending the indefensible."

Great. Malakh lets everybody off the hook except for me. Clarissa did it only with the pool guy. Brett he minimizes because the kid had to make a living; what, he couldn't wait on tables, drive a cab? He even tried to make Essie feel guilty about the old white guy and neither one was even married. Where does that leave me? I'm screwed because I screwed, it's my fault that God made me oversexed? Who asked Him to do that, did I make a special request for that? He loaded me up with testosterone, that's not my fault. No more apologies from me, *toujours de l'audace*; the best defense is an offense. It's time Malakh stopped picking on me, I've got feelings, too.

"Look," I say out loud, "I did what I did, it can't be undone. I can't lie and say I'm sorry; you'd know that I was lying anyway. What can I do now, it's too late. Maybe one of your angels should have had a heart-to-heart chat with me thirty years ago; now, it's too late. So I'd appreciate it if you'd change the subject, talk about something else. Leave the ladies out of it, enough is enough."

To my surprise, Malakh complies with my request.

"All right," he says. "I have to ask certain questions of each of you; they are part of a form I must fill out for the High Court. Everything is done by forms nowadays. We are inundated with souls and, much as I prefer the old ways, we have to conform to the process. The first question I need answered from each of you is what single thing would you have most wanted to change if you could live your life over again. One thing, now, answer as pithily as possible. Let's go in order. Clarissa, you first."

She replies immediately, with no hesitation.

"I would have tried harder to convince Andy to continue those miserable fertility treatments. I wouldn't have given up. I would have moved heaven and earth to have Andy's child, to give him that. I gave him plenty of happiness with Twinky, but it would have been complete the other way. I wouldn't have had to live with that lie."

Mendel is next.

"It's hard for me to say this. I think you expect me to talk about my father again but, no, something else bothers me even more. For what did I survive, for what did Luba survive, what did we each crawl out of that cursed Europe for? To run a candy store, to raise a boy who forgets his heritage and makes a lot of money, this is it? I think we should have lived differently, maybe we should have moved to Israel, we were afraid, we didn't want to live through another war.

But maybe there life would have had more meaning. Or we could have stayed in Europe, that bloody swamp, and tried to rebuild our community. But no, we ran, we ran away, and for what? To sell candy bars, bubble gum, the *Daily News*? For this I survived? Maybe we should have made such a choice, I think it would have been better. Avery would have been proud to call himself Abraham, maybe life would have been harder but sweeter."

Everybody looks at Brett, although I know what he's going to say, we all do. And sure enough, he states the obvious.

"I wouldn't have let my Dad learn about me. Somehow I would have prevented it; that's the mistake of my life. And once he did, I should have talked to him about it—not about the clients, never about them—but I should have tried to make him understand about my being gay. We never talked about it. He was supposed to love me; he was my father, damn it. Maybe we could have been friends again but I didn't have the courage. I always put it off. How am I going to face him even now, up here? Will he even meet with me, will he speak to me up here, do earthly fights continue up here? Malakh, will he be made to see me or can he turn away from me here, too? Malakh, what will he do?"

"Please," answers Malakh, "please don't ask me such details. I don't know. Much depends on the judgment. There are reunions, I already said that, but I don't know about each case. After the judgment, other angels take over, they escort you to your fates. I have enough problems here, don't ask me about later." Then he adds, turning to Essie, "Next."

"I would have stayed home and raised my boys, I wouldn't have worked while James was alive. We would have been poor, mighty poor, but I would have been there with them, not raising someone else's child. I raised Patsy, not my own flesh and blood; instead I would have kept an eye on Willy, kept him from his bad ways. Nothing I can do about it now, but the Lord knows I would change that if I could."

My turn. I know exactly what I would have changed.

"I haven't talked much about my son, Bobby," I begin. "I don't want to sound negative about him, I love him but maybe I loved him too much. Maybe because he is an only child, who knows, but I didn't do a great job with him, I didn't toughen him up for the world. I never sent him to work until he was out of college and even before that I smoothed his way through school. Money, that was probably the problem, too much money. You wouldn't think there could be too much, everybody wants more, but it's not so good for a kid, especially for a boy. I paid his way out of all kinds of scrapes, I never let him hit bottom, never let him worry. Not my little prince. And once in a while, when I tried to make some demands of him, Jane would jump to his defense, like a tigress, I shouldn't hurt his feelings, his precious feelings.

"All he had to do was look sad and, bingo, we jumped in to save him. He needed a job, Daddy found it for him. He wanted to marry, why should he wait until he could afford it? Daddy will help. Daddy, Daddy. Except now I'm dead and there is no Daddy, good old Daddy is history. Here I am, dead as a doornail, and I'm worrying whether he'll be able to cope down there without me. Although God knows he never really appreciated all I did for him; I don't think I ever got more than a polite thanks and that usually only when Jane reminded him. It was all coming to him, that's how we made him feel. Didn't Freud say that a man whose mother adored him will walk through life like a king? Something like that. King Bobby. God, I hope he can figure things out. I'm worried about him, I can't stop worrying about him. He's smart, sharp as a knife, he's good at numbers. Maybe my death will toughen him up, I hope so."

"Okay," says Malakh, "I've recorded everything. This is one of the most interesting parts of my job; every soul that passes through here has regrets, it fascinates me. What an interesting thing it must be to live down there, all those choices. It would drive me crazy. Me, all I've got to do is my job, no wife, no sex life, no earning a living, full room and board. I don't envy you people, it's tough down there. So, another question on the form, this gets some of the strangest answers. What are you proudest of about your earthly lives? No holding back now, the truth is what's needed. Don't give me the obvious, don't tell me about your children or your marriage here. I want to know what you think you did best. This is about you. Let's go, same order. Clarissa."

"Well don't belittle me for my answer; you may think I'm being silly but don't make light of what I'm about to say. My greatest talent was fashion, just the right outfit, the right fit. Okay, I made money from it, yes, I dealt with plenty of difficult women, but what I did was important. All those ladies who needed my help, sagging breasts, huge hips; I don't want to even remember what I've seen in the way of behinds and upper thighs. A chamber of horrors. And I had to make them look decent, find just the right outfit, just the right accessory to take the eye off the disaster area and emphasize whatever good existed. Do you realize all the miracles I performed? Veritable tanks made to look shapely, elephants repackaged and presented to the public as gazelles. Redesigned women who were able to attract men or look good at their daughter's wedding. One miracle after another, that was my talent. I was an artist, in my way just as good as Chagall or Picasso and just as innovative. And I had to work with raw material which was much more challenging. I think I improved life for many of my clients and I'm proud of it."

Malakh turns to Mendel, who shrugs.

"What, I should be proud of something? I sold newspapers, more people were able to read that *fashtunkeneh New York Times* because I sold it, that leftist rag. Or maybe the Lotto tickets I sold. Or the Hershey bars? To me, it's a silly question. What I was best at? At surviving, at not going mad, at not killing Germans after the war. At staying human. That's it, I'm proud of staying human."

Brett is ready with his answer.

"I made people happy, not my family, not Freddy maybe, but most of the others, most of those men. I gave them value. Maybe you think of me as just a lowlife but I gave value. Always smiling, always greeting them with warmth; so many of them were lonely, sad, pathetic. With me they turned into royalty, they were in charge. I pretended to adore them, I admired their manliness, I was a great courtesan. Some of you may despise me for it, but I'm proud of it. Everybody got their money's worth from me."

Essie's turn.

"I'm proud of my faith. I believe in the mercy of the Lord; I kept my faith strong, I believed even when I was low, even when the devil got his hands on me. Even when James and Willy died, I was like a rock. I held on when I was tried by the good Lord. Mac used to say to me, 'Hold on, be strong, you're like a tree with deep roots, no wind can blow you down.' Mac said that and it was true. Maybe I shouldn't boast but it's the God's honest truth. Lord knows, I held firm, thank you, Jesus."

And now it's me, what the hell can I say about myself? I might as well tell the truth, Malakh will know if I lie. So here goes.

"Me? I wasn't loaded with talent, I was pretty ordinary. But I was desperate, one thing I knew, I didn't want to end up like my poor father, dying while dragging himself to work to pay the rent. Not me. What did I do best? I made money. I got rich, not hundreds of millions, but plenty rich. Rich is a lot better than the alternative, let me tell you. I was rolling in money and, you know what, everybody treated me right because of it. People relied on me, they needed me. The only people who think that money is not important are people with lots of it. So that's it for me. I was best at making money, call me *pisher*, but that's it."

Boy, that felt good to say, that's my unvarnished truth, let them like it or not.

"Wow," says Malakh, "those were all great responses. We're getting good here, you're all getting into the rhythm of this thing, we're doing fine. I have one more mandatory question. Don't ask me why the Court wants this one but they do: how do you envision God, how do you see Him? No fancy replies here; give me the truth, your visceral response. C'mon."

"A distant figure, father-like," says Clarissa. "Merciful."

"He turned away," says Mendel. "He created us and then He washed His hands of us. He stopped caring, if He really exists at all."

Brett responds. "Harsh," he says, "always testing us, pushing us around, punishing us when we fail. Sometimes He's so cruel. Sometimes He seems to be a bully."

"Oh, no," objects Essie, "you mustn't feel that way. He's all love but we're not wise enough to understand His ways. He's not cruel, Lord have mercy, He's all love."

Everybody looks at me, what in the world can I say, I'm going to sound like a simpleton.

"An old man with a white beard. I'm sorry, I know it sounds dumb, but that's what I think. Like an old rabbi, that's the way I see him."

"All right," says Malakh, "we're finished with the formal part of the process. I will now ascend to the next sphere and find out about your scheduling for judgment. Before I go, are there any questions?"

"Yes," says Clarissa. "I see my body, I see my clothes, even the wonderful pink bag, one of my favorites. But they were all shredded, torn to bits in the accident and yet they look fine now. But I can't feel them, they have no weight. And I can't really seem to move. What's happened?"

"All of you still carry your body images with you but these are simply illusions. You have exited your bodies; these images are retained to help you adjust. At the end of the seventh day they will begin to fade away and all that will ultimately remain will be your essences. Meanwhile, don't try to use them."

"I'll never have my body again?" asks Brett. "I worked so hard on it, to keep it fit, to make it beautiful. I'm not saying it was perfect but it sure was close. Hours of hard work, people admiring it, and it's gone? That's terrible, I don't know how to cope with that."

Malakh replies in a surprisingly gentle tone. "It's not just your bodies you all have to say goodbye to, it's everything. It's your relationships, it's your emotions, it's even most of your memories, which will fade. The only item that will remain is the feeling of loyalty to those you loved. All else will fade, is really already fading. These seven days begin this process; after the thirty days of judgment all else will disappear, all but your essence and your bodily illusion. I know it must be difficult for you to accept, and frightening, but that is your fate, the fate of all mankind. You must trust that this is all for the best. Your parents and ancestors have all preceded you through the identical path; you may find comfort in that. But now you must concentrate on the judgment, you must face the Judge. Tremble and prepare, you must pass before the Judgment Throne like everyone else, one by one."

I can see that the others are as shocked as I feel, it's evident in their expressions. I don't know how much of the seven days are left, and why the judgment would take thirty days. I don't get it.

Malakh looks at me intently. I don't even have to ask the question, he knows.

"I cannot reveal more of the nature of the process; what I've said is all I can talk about. Each step on the way, there will be guidance provided, but no more now. Now you must surrender your sense of control and submit to the inevitable process. You must proceed to judgment with as little sense of what will occur as you had when you were alive. I can advise you no more."

"That's incredibly cruel," interjects Brett. "Why such cruelty? Okay, so life was tough and sometimes miserable, but I would have thought that up here things would be kinder, less chaotic. I object. I think this stinks. We spill out our hearts and souls to you and then you drift away without answering all of our questions, without comforting us. I don't get it and I object."

"What did you expect," snorts Mendel, "you expected kindness? Kindness you shouldn't hope for, don't expect a stone to sing."

"Why shouldn't you guide us further?" I ask of Malakh. "You're giving us the bum's rush, you're pushing us through too fast, you want the next batch of souls to come through. You should tell us whatever you know, try to make is easier for us. Not so fast, Malakh."

I can see that Essie is horrified.

"That's an angel," she reminds us, "be careful what you say."

"Angel, shmangel," replies Mendel. "Better he should be aggravated than we should be."

Clarissa tries charm. "Please don't abandon us now, Malakh. I won't know where to turn without you."

What an operator she is, but Malakh remains stern, stone-faced.

"Sorry," he says, "it is good for you that you should be fearful, that you should tremble. Then maybe you will approach this judgment with the gravity it deserves."

"But Malakh," Clarissa pleads, "think how difficult our lives have been. We've all made mistakes, we all have regrets. Why not hold our hands here, help us through. You promised you would; it isn't fair."

"I can go no further with you," he replies. "You are on your own now, you must prepare your own defenses. I'm not your lawyer here, I'm an angel and not a very high level one at that. I've done my part. I wish you all the best but I have souls waiting and I've got to move on."

"And what if we refuse?" I ask. "What if we will not submit to this judgment? Who will make us? Life stank, maybe the judgment will, too. Who needs it, why should we agree? Let us out of here without it, a bunch of angels or whatever sitting in judgment over us. Judges who may never have lived on earth, never been tempted, never suffered, it isn't fair. How can that be just? These guys were never tempted by a beautiful woman, they never had to pay the rent, nobody ever yelled at them, mistreated them. What the hell do they know about the pain, about the needs? No, it's not fair."

Mendel jumps in. "That's the truth, I hear the truth here. My father used to sing a song, 'In this world, agony and sighing, in the next world, Sabbath peace.' So where is the peace? Here also we must suffer. It isn't decent; you should hold each of our hands, not abandon us. These judges of yours, any of them live through Auschwitz? Any of these angel judges watch their world burn all around them? Who are they to sit in judgment, what do they know? Who are they? We should be entitled to know."

"No, you are not," replies Malakh somewhat abruptly. "You have no entitlements. And who are you? Nothings and nobodies, flesh and blood, bits of souls stuffed into disposable bodies. Like a dream, you float away, you're fragile, of little consequence. You want the right to decide who will judge you? Is this a joke or temporary insanity or what? Such a nerve. I haven't encountered such an outrage ever before. You'd better calm down here, revolutions are not permitted here. Essie, you'd better talk to your friends here, calm them down."

Essie does not immediately reply. I can see in her face

that she is conflicted, she's not such an easy target as Malakh thought.

Finally, she opines. "I'm not sure I agree with you, Malakh. I'm sorry but I don't know what to think. I'd like to know who these judges are, too. Did they ever have to wrestle with the devil, did they ever feel hungry, did people ever look at them with contempt, laugh at them, spit at them? Did they ever have to bury a loved one? Lord knows, I've done that. I'd like to know that. I hope you don't mind."

"Have you all lost your minds?" asks a now angry Malakh. "This is a first. I've had really tragic cases here and nobody acted this way before. Who instigated this? Is it you, Irv? I think it's you. Big man, huh? Big shot. Well, not up here, here you're just another soul, another petty soul, a no one and a nothing like all the rest."

Clarissa dives in. "If we're such nothings, why are we judged? Why should any of you care about interrogating us, why does it matter? I don't think so. I think we matter a lot, I think we are exactly what matters most. I'm not cooperating until I know what's next. I refuse, so there. And I don't believe for even one minute that we are the first to feel this way. I wasn't born yesterday. We're not the first and we won't be the last."

"Of course, we're not. Plenty of people must have fought back," agrees Mendel, "and I can tell you, Malakh, I'm not moving from this place, I'm not lifting a finger until I'm satisfied. Otherwise, I'm staying here; let them bring the Court here if they want; they should live and be healthy, but I'm not moving."

Here's Brett again. "Look at me," he says, "I'm about to be judged, maybe they'll disapprove of me, okay, I sold my body. But who made me this way, did I choose to be gay? Look at me. Who put my soul into this body? Does it seem right to you? Six feet two, shoulders of a weight lifter, me Tarzan *and* Jane! Did I do this to myself? Why should I be judged for it? It isn't right, it's just not."

Mendel again. "Doesn't it say in our books, 'Will the Judge of the whole earth not do justice?' Didn't someone ask that?"

"I think it was Abraham in the Bible, he said that," adds Essie.

"Yes, right, it was Abraham and he had the courage to say that, to ask that. If it was good enough for him, what, I shouldn't also ask such a question?" responds Mendel.

"Enough already!" shouts Malakh. "I've heard enough. Stop yelling, you can yell from now until the cows come home but it won't help. I'm leaving. I'll be back in a little while. Meanwhile, think about what you're doing here, have a little caucus here, get smart."

And he disappears. The light leaves with him; we are cast into darkness. It shakes me up, it scares me. I suppose it's meant to. After a little while I can begin to see the other faces again. Mendel speaks.

"Don't be afraid," he urges us. "Don't let him scare us with the dark. Get used to it, think of it as your friend. In Auschwitz, I was always safer in the dark; it can be useful, you can hide in it."

Clarissa responds. "I'm not at all afraid, not at all. If there is no justice even up here, if this is just a repetition of what we lived through down there, then I don't care anymore. Let them do their worst to me, I just don't care."

"I thought I'd see my baby, my Willy, and James, of course, and Mac. And my momma and my daddy. I thought they'd be waiting for me with a hug and with a kiss. I never thought it would be like this, another long row to hoe, more hard labor. I don't mean to judge the Lord, but this is plain not nice. I'm very disappointed."

"You'll be fine, Essie," says Brett. "Don't worry, they'll whisk you through, you were a fine person. I've got to worry, maybe Irv, but not you."

I look at the kid with new admiration, he's got backbone, he's okay.

"Why thank you," replies Essie, "thank you for those kind words. Please, everybody, be so kind, join me as I recite David's psalm, you all know it, please join me."

"'The Lord is my shepherd, I shall not want. He maketh me to lie down in green pastures, He leadeth me beside the still waters, He restoreth my soul. He guideth me in straight paths for His name's sake.'" She stops, she looks around. "Oh, I'm so sorry, I forgot the next line, I forgot. I'm used to reading it from my Bible and I've just plumb forgotten."

Clarissa pitches in. "'Yea, though I walk through the valley of the shadow of death I will fear no evil for Thou art with me, Thy rod and Thy staff, they comfort me. Thou preparest a table before me. . . .'"

But we are interrupted.

Part III

Angels

A nother angel, glowing with sharp beams of light, enters our space. He has a severe expression on his face, annoyed, petulant. We all float about in absolute silence as he eyes each of us. Finally, he speaks, his voice raspy.

"I am the angel Kataygore and you are, I am informed, the troublesome lot from Park and Fifty-seventh. Don't want to be judged, eh? You refuse judgment; right, that's what I'm told."

No one replies. This angel is intimidating.

"You," he says, pointing to me, "you must be Irv, that great humanitarian who doesn't require repentance, the instigator of the rebellion. You, a vulgarian who used his blessing of wealth for self-indulgence, a womanizer, a bum. Maybe we should open a special path for you; whoremasters should be let in without any fuss. The celestial choir should perform for you. Maybe we can even find some girls for you, at no charge, of course."

Kataygore turns to Clarissa.

"And you, sweet little you, selling your soul so you could buy clothes and jewelry, you with two feet and at least seventy pairs of shoes. Not to mention the carefully selected matching handbags. You who got your jollies from the point of purchase, from the right scarf, happiness blessed by Saint Manolo Blahnik or that holy spirit Loro Piana. You, who jumped on a nineteen-year-old boy to father your Twinky, your great gift to mankind, a tennis-playing world-class shopper. This is the heritage you have bequeathed to future generations."

"And you," pointing at Brett, "little Mr. Goody Two-Shoes, that great benefactor of gay mankind, the man with the perfectly sculpted behind, perfect pecs, available for a few hundred an hour. Too delicate to work from nine to five, too sensitive for such a pedestrian lifestyle. You were so spreadable it's incredible."

He's looking around.

"Oh, there's Essie. The Lord this, the Lord that. Thank you, Jesus. Right, but when it comes to the real thing, the moment of judgment you've been praying and singing about all your life, no thanks. You don't want it, you're too good for it. It's okay to swipe a little jewelry, you had to eat; it's okay to hate that employer of yours, that Mrs. Perry. Remember how you wished her ill, remember? Well, *we* do. But you don't need to be judged, you're too good. Well, thank the Lord!

"And then there's Mendel. You know, you left Auschwitz more than sixty years ago. How about changing your tune? Enough already, sixty years of complaining, you drove your son away with your endless grieving. And you knew damned well that you ate your father's food, that you let him starve to death to save you. And now you're trying to reconcile

with him, to remember him lovingly. Well, dead fathers are
easy to love, they can't annoy you anymore. Stop lying to
yourself and put all that behind you. Why should you be
exempt from judgment?"

A blistering, withering string of attacks. I am shivering,
I feel scared, I feel hurt, I feel angry. Mostly, I feel angry.
I look around at the others; they didn't deserve this.
Maybe I do, but not them, not Essie, not Mendel.

"No," I blurt out, "you have no right to say that. Shut
your mouth, stop right there. What is this, a good guy–bad
guy act? We're killed in an instant, no time to prepare,
whisked up here, interrogated, our little secrets pried out of
us, and then we are hustled off to a judgment we're not prepared for. No. And no again. I'm not going. Okay, I liked the
ladies, I cheated on my wife, I was a whoremaster. What do
you know? Were you ever down there in that snake pit, did
you ever feel lost and lonely, did you watch your father die
of overwork, did you ever actually work for a boss yourself?
Were you ever poor, bone poor, did you ever haul your ass
to work with a fever, start your own businesses from scratch?
Who the hell are you to speak to me that way? Get your ass
down there, try being a human being for fifty or sixty or seventy years and then we'll talk. Until then, keep your distance
from me."

I look around, Essie is crying, so is Brett. Not Clarissa.

"How dare you," she begins, "how dare you speak to us

in that tone. You belittle my life, what can you understand of it? I may have been silly about clothes, I certainly did commit adultery with one man, maybe you don't like what I did about Twinky, but never, never ever did I speak with such contempt and with such venom as you just did to us. You're an evil thing, you're twisted. I will not deal with the likes of you. I never shamed anyone like you're trying to shame us. I'm a lady, I was brought up to be a lady, but if I could spit, I would spit on you."

Brett is emboldened although his face is streaked with tears.

"I don't want to waste too much breath on you," he says quietly. "I'll answer for my lifestyle only to God, not to you, not to any angel, not to any judge. He created me, He made me what I am, He made me with this face and with this body and with certain needs. I won't answer to you for anything I've done, I'll answer only to Him."

And he turns away, averts his eyes from Kataygore.

Mendel has been absolutely still. His face betrays no evident emotion. Now he speaks. "Let me see this God of yours, let me hear from Him. Because so far He's just a theory. Now He wants me to be judged. Now He is suddenly interested? Not when they murdered our six million, not when they slaughtered millions in Soviet Russia, not in Rwanda. Certainly not in Auschwitz where the beasts ruled, where games were played with the lives of inmates, if you were fourth in line you lived, fifth you died. One more needed for the gas chamber? You, you go, you don't. And they laughed, those Germans, what fun they had. And I should forget, why remember? But you see, Mr. Big Shot Angel, for me the children are still screaming, the women are still shrieking. And now, in Israel, evil ones are again trying to kill my people, terrorists with bombs. And doesn't God give those murderers oil, doesn't it spout out of God's earth and pay for the bombs? It is dangerous to forget Auschwitz, it is safer to remember. As to my father, maybe you are right. I was young, I wanted to live, but I will not explain to you. You are not worthy to even mention my father's name, he was a holy man. You, you are an evil spirit with a filthy mouth. I rebuke you."

I tense up, ready for another volley but Kataygore stands motionless, silent. His expression is belligerent, cold. A very long time passes in this way and then with no warning, he is gone and we are back in the dark. No one says a word and yet I can feel the emotions that unite us. For the first time I feel truly close to these people. We are all in the same boat. Before I can collect my thoughts, here's Malakh again, light surrounds him and he is smiling kindly at us

"I'm back," he says. "I saw that Kataygore paid you a visit. I hope you found it useful; he's very well connected up here. I hope you sent him away satisfied. He's close to the Boss."

I know Malakh can read my mind but now I'm reading his. This is a good cop–bad cop ploy, Kataygore beats us up and sweet Malakh returns to mop up.

"Malakh," I say, "you know precisely what we said to him, stop treating us like children. I for one, refuse to submit, I want to know who the judges are, I want you to tell us what each of us is going to face. I'm tired of your little lowly angel act, ignorant little you. Stop the bullshit and tell us what we need to know."

Malakh's smile is gone. At least I've done that, erased that grin from his face. His eyes go steely as he rivets them on me.

"You didn't have enough?" he asks, "you want more? Here, take a look, it's your wife and her mother, oh, about ten years ago."

I see Jane and her mother, Ruth, having coffee at the Palm Court in the Plaza Hotel. Jane is leaning forward, her demeanor quite serious, her voice urgent.

"I can't stand it anymore, Mom, I can't bear it. Another business trip, now to Rome. He carefully planned it to coincide with Bobby's oral surgery so I can't go. There's no business there, only monkey business. That's his third trip there in two years. Not to mention all his evening business appointments here in New York. Nobody seems to have business meetings during daylight hours anymore. I can't stand it; he's spitting in my eye, he's out of control. I've got to teach him a lesson."

"No, Jane, if you mean you want a divorce, you can't do it, you'll break Bobby's heart, he loves Irv. You've got to wait until he's grown, you can't do it now. Irv isn't mean or rude to your face, he's not abusive. You have to live with it, you can't be selfish at Bobby's expense. Don't even think about it, put it out of your mind."

"I can't anymore, it's so blatant. He obviously either thinks I'm an idiot or that I'm so weak that I won't dare confront him. Either way, he's insulting me. I don't want to look at him anymore."

"Please," says Ruth, "I don't want to hear any more of this nonsense. Bobby comes first, you know that. Take it out on Irv in other ways, buy things you want, be extravagant, buy jewelry, make him pay that way."

"I'm not interested in any of that, you know that, Mom. I've got copies of all his financial records, I know where every penny is. I could take him and wring him out, leave him with squat. That's what he deserves. I'm beginning to hate him."

"I forbid it, Jane. Don't you do this, not as long as I'm alive. Put your feelings aside, squelch them. Let the animal have his fun but protect your child. You want revenge? You're an attractive woman, have a nice affair yourself, you've got my permission. While he's dragging his whore through Rome, get busy. What about that ENT man you go to with Bobby? I took Bobby twice, he's a handsome man, so nice. He asked me so many questions about you. I'm sure he's interested. There are plenty of fish in the sea. Start fishing, that's my advice. And a few diamonds wouldn't hurt either; he wouldn't dare say anything, even he wouldn't have the nerve."

The picture fades. I look at Malakh. I'd like to find out, did she? I don't think so but I'd sure like to know. But I'm not giving him the satisfaction, I'm not asking. Look how he's looking at me, waiting for me to beg. Shove it up your ass, if you have one. You won't get me to beg. So Jane knew. My God, I wonder how she really feels about my death. I wonder if she's relieved.

Now he's smirking at me, he knows. I turn away. I wouldn't like to think that Jane is happy I'm gone. I don't believe it. Look how she sent me for blue shirts, she cared how I looked. She still loved me, I know she did. You're not going to aggravate me, Malakh, I'm not going to let you. She wanted to bring out the blue of my eyes; she loved me. But what did I do to her, she didn't deserve to be dishonored that way. I thought I was so clever, every little lie so carefully devised, those trips mixed in with just enough business to make them look genuine. If I had known that she was wise to me I wouldn't have done all that, I wouldn't have dared. Our lives would have been different. Maybe I wouldn't be floating here now out of my mind about the judgment.

"Shall I continue, folks?" asks Malakh. "Shall we delve further? Should I remind you, Clarissa, that after Donny left for school at the end of that summer, you, shall we say, stalked him a little? Called him, wanted him to let you know whether he would be back in town to visit his parents. Bought him shirts, ties, showered him with gifts. A watch, cuff links. Good old Andy never noticed. Oh, and Brett, maybe you'd like to tell us about your client Tommy. He was a steady client, wasn't he, the one you used to put on a tutu for? Didn't he prefer you in a very particular position while wearing that tutu? Maybe you'd like to describe it for the folks. Good old Tommy Whitty, he always liked the ballet."

"Tommy Whitty! What do you mean?" shouts Clarissa. "That was my first husband, Tommy. Oh, you must be wrong. This is a cruel joke, I don't believe you, Malakh. I don't believe that of Tommy."

She looks at Brett, asks what he looks like.

"Tommy is around sixty, blonde hair, blue eyes. Oh! He's got a squarish birthmark on his right shoulder."

"Oh, God," she says, "it *is* Tommy."

She turns back to Malakh.

"You knew all along, you were laughing at me all along. What's going on here? We're perfect strangers here and yet my Tommy was his lover and my worst enemy had an affair with Irv. Something strange is going on here. What is it, Malakh? You know something, what is it?"

No reply.

We all look at Malakh, his face reveals nothing.

"There is so much more that happens in your world that you don't know, don't understand," he says to us. "All of you humans are like sleepwalkers; you move about and most of the time you are unaware of what you are doing. There are realms of existence you cannot even dream of, reincarnations and judgments that take place without your knowledge. Things occur in your world to correct what happened in previous lives. It is not as chaotic, as accidental, as it all seems down there. Why try to understand? Just give in to the inevitable. I'll do you all a favor, I'll see if the Court can take you right away. You won't have to wait thirty days. How about it?"

We are all silent. Maybe some of the others are weakening but not me. I won't be whipped into submission.

"Remember," adds Malakh, "the longer you wait, the more time to dredge up evidence against you, to recall more events that might not reflect well on you. Delay is not to your advantage."

Clarissa replies. "Something has brought us together; it is clearly not all chance. Let's stick together, let's get tough here. Malakh, I'm not submitting to more of this until I know more. I agree that much of life is not understandable but that was down there. Now I want to be made to understand, I want my life to be given some

meaning even if it must be in retrospect. Otherwise, I'm
not budging."

"Fine," answers Malakh, "then don't budge. As I look
at it, you, Essie, and you, Mendel, led fairly exemplary, if
painful, lives. I probably should have put you two on the
fast track for a quick judgment. Reunions await you, con-
solations await you. Why don't the two of you submit to
the judgment, let the others take their sweet time? Why
should you suffer? I'm trying to help you here, Essie, what
do you say?"

"Good Lord, what kind of a person do you think I am?"
Essie retorts. "First you talk sweet to us, then you send that
lowdown nasty angel to scream at us, and now you're trying
to separate us. Well, shame on you, I'm not paying you any
mind anymore. You turn around now and just go. I'll wait
right here for the Lord Himself. I've waited on Him all my
life long and I'm expecting Him, I'm expecting a miracle.
So go along now, leave me be."

Malakh doesn't even wait to hear whether Mendel will
reply.

"I'm going," he says, "but before I do, I want to remind
you that you are not exactly a band of saints, you don't reek
of righteousness. Essie, you waited for the Lord, right?
Always waiting on Him. How then would you explain the
way you treated Mrs. Perry as she lay dying of cancer? You
took care of her, but coldly, never with a smile, everything

done mechanically. You hated her, didn't you? You hated her guts. Do you think the Lord approves of envy like that? She paid you, she didn't cheat you, maybe you didn't like her, but why the hatred, why the envy? She was dying, for Heaven's sake, couldn't you spare her some of that mercy you now want for yourself? Where was all that love you talk about?"

Essie is clearly taken aback; she stumbles over her reply.

"She was a mean woman, Lord forgive me. She lorded it over Mr. Perry, never had a kind word for my Patsy. To me she was cruel, all those years of my hard labor and never a thank you, never a word of praise. But I did my duty. I washed her, I cooked for her, I never said a nasty word back to her, never, as the Lord is my witness, but I sure couldn't love her. So that's my sin, is it? Well, I *am* guilty of that. Maybe I've been punished for it, I buried my James and my Willy. Maybe I was punished but long ago I repented; God alone knows that I prayed for pardon. But you know, in that mean world down there, feeling the way I did, I tried my best but I just couldn't try to make her happy. God Himself doesn't make most people happy, so how could He expect us to, we're just dust and ashes."

Malakh turns to Brett.

"Remember that camping scene you seem to blame everything on? Your description of what happened was a little off the mark. You were old enough to recall more than you described; memories can play tricks. Are you sure that counselor jumped on top of you? Maybe if you try hard you'll remember your crawling into his sleeping bag. He was fast asleep; it was you who made the first move, it was you who started the ball rolling. You want me to get graphic here or is your memory improving? Shall I bring back the visual, play it out? You want us all to see what really happened, who seduced whom?"

"I don't believe you! That's a lie. I remember it clearly; he started, not me. I swear that's the way it was. I was an innocent kid, it wasn't even something I imagined. I don't care what you do."

And the visual is brought up. It was pitch black in the tent but we all see Brett leave his sleeping bag and approach the other boy. We see him waking the other fellow up with his vigorous touch, climbing on top of him. Brett can bear no more.

"Stop, please stop. I swear I remember it the other way around, I swear on all that's holy. Maybe this is rigged. I remember it so clearly. Please, stop it. Please, have a little mercy here, please."

But Malakh doesn't stop and we see more. One by one, we turn away, we avert our faces, we close our eyes. We will not join in his humiliation.

"So what," I say, "so what? Who cares? He was a young kid, so he started. What does that have to do with anything?

Leave him alone. We're expected to be so kind and good on earth, never hurt someone's feelings, and didn't you lecture us before about not shaming anyone? And look at you, what are you doing? There are no rules, no limits? What kind of place is this, what kind of creature are you?"

Clarissa interjects, "A damned nasty one, that's what he is. Who would have guessed that dying is like going from the frying pan into the fire? At least on earth people pretend to be nice; they smile at you, wish you good morning, and *then* try to cut your throat. Here there are no preliminaries, right to your jugular. You just make me angry. I can't believe you're permitted to act like this."

"And you," Malakh says to her, "didn't you forget to mention just one little fact? Good old Andy, he wasn't as permissive about your spending habits as you would have us believe, was he? Remember those fights about your bills? Remember those twelve and thirteen thousand dollar clothing bills? Those alligator shoes you bought in six colors, the ones with the little gold and crystal beads that cost over a thousand a pair? So what did you do, Clarissa, and how many times did you do it? I believe the word is shoplifting, isn't it? Didn't you wear old shoes into the store on many occasions, put on new ones, throw out the old, and stroll out in the new? And then there were the bills you hid and paid in cash, cash you took from Andy's pocket slowly and carefully so he wouldn't notice, over the course of time.

Wait until Andy finds the latest batch in your night table. You were an addict, a shopaholic, Clarissa. Twinky was not the only secret you kept from him."

"Big deal," I interject, "what a calamity. She must be the only woman ever who kept bills from her husband, a unique phenomenon. Boy, you had to dig deep to come up with something that picayune. Give me a break."

"Oh," says Malakh, "Irv expresses his opinion, another province is heard from. And what a judge of morality you make. I won't repeat my mention of that underage girl you were busy with for quite some time, but maybe the folks would like to see some visuals of you in the back of your car keeping company with ladies who charge twenty-five for a few minutes of their time. How democratic of you. You were never a snob; as long as they were female and breathing, it was fine with you. A man of the people. You should be proud. And remember when your wife was away at a convention? Well, I seem to recall your spending time with that neighbor of yours. You do remember Lavinia, right? The two of you in your bed, the bed you shared with Jane. How nice, the idea of love your neighbor brought to new levels. And in Jane's bed. One thing I have to say for you, you had your housekeeper change the sheets before Jane returned. You were always very clean."

Mendel jumps in. "Enough already, Mr. Angel, enough with all these sex scenes. What, are you frustrated, it pleases you to see all this dirt? You should be ashamed. Aren't we in a holy place here? This is not a porno movie theater. For shame."

"Okay Mendel, maybe you're right, maybe I'm digging around in too much dirt here. Fine. But with you I'll be clean, no dirt with you, you were faithful to Luba, never strayed. Congratulations. However, never once, not even once in all the years since Auschwitz, not once a word of thanks to the God who made you, not a word of prayer after those few times you said the Kaddish for your father. Couldn't spare the time, I suppose, too busy selling the papers and the bubble gum. On your train from Gyor, almost four hundred people and you were one of only fifteen to survive. No gratitude, just complaints, just bitterness. Sixty years of it. You took your father's food in the camp. What did you think, he bought that stray potato or turnip in a grocery store, in a supermarket? You realized that he was starving himself and did you care? Who are you to reject God's judgment, who are you to demur? Everyone is given a certain life, yours was hard, I understand. But who are you to question, to reject? Who do you think you are?"

"Me, I know who I am. Do you? You fly around, annoying and toying with souls, no risk for you, no dangers, no temptations. Who are you or your kind to judge me? I was young. When you are young you hunger for life, you want to miss nothing. Of course I knew we were all starving, sure I saw my father withering away. I was so hungry, it was hard to turn down food. Many fathers did similar things or more. A few weeks before liberation at the morning roll call, one of the Germans selected a father and his son to step forward. They were the Rosensteins from our town. I knew the son from our school. Everybody knew how close they were, how devoted one to the other. I suppose the Germans saw it, too, and decided to have some fun.

"The officer said to them that they had to fight against each other with their fists and the loser would be shot. They said no, they would not hit each other. 'Fine, then you will die together right now, right here,' the German said and took out his gun. The father turned to the boy and ordered him in Hungarian to hit hard, to knock him down, to knock him unconscious. The boy refused. 'I order you, I command you,' said the father. 'I order you to live; honor me and do what I say. Hit me and do it hard, knock me unconscious, honor me. Hurry.' And he did, the boy did that as hard as he could to lessen the suffering. The father was down, bleeding; again he ordered his son, 'Finish me, hurry.' And he did. When the German walked over to shoot the father he patted the boy on his back. 'Good job,' he said and laughed. This is what a father will do for his child, this is the world we found ourselves in. And you feel you can judge me."

"What happened to the boy, did he make it, did he survive?" asks Clarissa.

"The next day he threw himself on the electric wire fence and died," answers Mendel. "Tell me, Angel, should anyone be so treated, should anyone have to live through such a thing? And if we are made to, is anyone to judge us if we emerge from that swamp of a world? What you are accusing all of us here of is nothing, of no importance. Be quiet now, you've done your worst, leave us in peace. It's too late for me anyway, there's no hope for me to be happy again. I wanted to see my family again, my Luba, but if not, not. You want to punish me, go ahead, do your worst. I am weary of you."

Malakh looks at him, a peculiar look on his face. Am I imagining it or do I see a flash of sympathy in his eyes? Who knows? As he floats away, we are again surrounded by darkness. I don't know about the others but I welcome it. It's all right, I could manage this way, just floating like this, left alone. And slowly I drift off into something like sleep. It must be some time before I am shaken into alertness by a sound. I see that the others are awakening, too. The light returns in a muted way and a very young angel floats by, I guess a cherub, he's got two small wings and a plump little body. A baby's body with a shrewd little face.

"I'm Seth," he announces in a soft voice. "You are each permitted to be visited by the soul of one person whose death preceded yours; this is a special concession because of your fears of judgment. Remember, just one, and only for a few seconds. And you may not speak, not one word. I work in the Reunions area and we're overwhelmed with needy souls, so please cooperate and be quick. Who wants to begin?"

Mendel responds. "I'd like to see my father, Abraham Perlow of Gyor in Hungary."

"Done," replies Seth, and we all see Mendel's father emerge from the cloudy surroundings. The man does not seem to have aged since we saw the pictures of him in Gyor but his body is ethereal, vague, faded. Mendel floats, mesmerized by the vision.

"Mendel, my Mendel," says the visitor, "I've been waiting for you. We have much to talk about. Here we have only the memory, the illusion of a body but we can still be recognized by our loved ones; it's so many years ago but you remember. Don't be afraid, son, Mama is waiting, Leah, too. You lived, you survived, you reached old age. This is our revenge on the murderers, that you had a son and grandsons. And those words of Kaddish, each was like a jewel to me, each word precious."

Mendel floats quietly as his father's image begins to fade and is gone.

Essie cries out. "My Willy, can I see my boy?"

Almost instantly a young black man's image appears. "Momma, it didn't hurt, I never felt a thing. I was dozing, the hum of the truck motor, I never felt it, Momma, I left your world just like that, in my sleep. Dad and I have kept an eye on you and Charlie, we've visited you, we were at Charlie's wedding."

And he fades away.

I wait for Clarissa and for Brett. Myself, I don't know who to ask for. My father died so long ago and my mother, will she resent me for putting her into the nursing home? I felt I had no choice, I was busy and she was slipping. She couldn't move in with us, that would have been too hard on Jane. Jane would have had to be with her all day. It wouldn't have been fair. I put her into the best place, it cost a fortune. She was so confused, but one thing she knew, she didn't want to leave her home. Over and over, she wanted to go home. What could I do, she didn't know the date, she didn't remember her address. What could I do?

Brett speaks up. "My mother, I choose her. But will she be herself again, will she be like before the Alzheimer's, will she know me?"

As he finishes the question, she appears. "It's me, Brett. Of course I know you. You were my strength, you were my rock, you gave me a feeling of safety as I weakened. You were my trust, I was safe with you. Don't be afraid, there's nothing to be afraid of."

Brett closes his eyes and bows his head. Clarissa looks at me.

"Go ahead." I say. "You go before me."

"My mother," she requests. "I didn't ever tell her about the affair, I need to hear from her."

The apparition looks strikingly like Clarissa, but with neatly arranged gray hair.

"I know all about it, dear, up here we see it all. I don't know what the fuss is about, you've brought up a splendid young woman who will in her turn bring up two grand-children for you. Andy will live to see that. You left a good legacy. Don't be too bothered as the angels pick away at you; it's their job in the seven days after death, it's not personal."

And she is gone. The cherub turns to me, what should I do? I can't face my mother, I can't. And what could my poor father have to say to me, he'll be angry at me, too. He was always very protective of her. One of the few opportunities I had to do something unselfish and I mucked it up.

"I'll skip it," I say. "No thanks, I'll wait until I'm with them, so I can explain. Right now, I can't handle it."

The others look at me. A wave of sympathy emanates from them. Essie would hug me hard if she could; her empathy is palpable. There are tears in Clarissa's eyes. I don't want their pity.

"You don't have to feel sorry for me," I claim. "I lived my life the way I wanted to, I'm willing to take the consequences."

Seth shrugs his fat little shoulders.

"It's fine with me," he says, "one less soul to dust off, bring here, and then return to its place."

And off he floats, taking the light with him. The others are all looking at me, I know what's on their minds. Seeing their families has taken the wind out of their sails, they're probably ready to go through the judgment. I've got to free them of their promise to hold together, it wouldn't be fair of me to hold them to it. I'm on my own, and I probably deserve it. Afraid to face my own parents, what a commentary on my life.

"Listen," I whisper, "you people go ahead without me. I'm not ready yet but you are, you'll all be okay. Go ahead, now, I'll be fine. Call for Malakh, tell him you're ready and good luck to you all."

The others are silent for quite some time. Then Clarissa objects.

"Come with us, Irv, don't even hesitate, you need to come with us. Maybe all our merits and demerits sort of cancel each other out. Maybe you and I and Brett need Essie and Mendel in our group so we can make it through. Me and my mountain of shoes and bags, Brett with his men, you with the ladies—maybe we were combined with the others to help us, to get us to the other side. Come with us, we won't let you go. You wouldn't leave us, would you?"

I have to tell them the truth, I have to explain how I feel. I'm afraid of how my own parents will receive me. They didn't have an extra penny but when my grandma took sick my mother took her in. I slept in the living room for three years because she lived with us until she died and you know what, I didn't think twice about it. It was my grandma. But years later I was rolling in dough, I could have kept my mother in her home, hired nurses; sure it would have cost hundreds of thousands and I would have been responsible if a nurse didn't show up. I was a busy man, I had to run my businesses, I had family responsibilities, I had to get laid. I needed some fun, too, what about me? These are good people; Essie and Mendel are saints, I can't even relate to them. Brett seems to have redeemed himself and as for Clarissa, what is she guilty of, a shoe fetish? And I'm lower than whale shit; those few good deeds I did were so unimportant to me I hardly remembered them.

"Go ahead, guys, don't wait for me," I say. "It's okay, go ahead. I'm not worthy to be with you; I hadn't realized it before, but I'm not worthy to shine your shoes. I'll stay here, don't worry about me."

And for the first time that I can remember since my mother died, tears come unbidden to my eyes and fall down my cheeks. I turn away so they won't see them, I try to hide my tears from them in the dark. Why should they suffer on my account?

I am stunned to hear a voice, not one I recognize, a mellow, deep voice which announces, "Some people win their eternity in one instant."

I open my eyes but I see no one, it's too dark. The voice continues.

"On earth, repentance, prayer, and charity can win pardon. Here it is too late for everything except repentance, but for repentance, the gate doesn't close until the very last second."

Did the others hear it, too, or just me? There is total silence. I shudder and close my eyes, let me be. The angels have won bringing that little fat angel in with loved ones who broke our ranks and it looks like the ballgame is over. Well, they've been doing this stuff for thousands of years, they know all the tricks. I'll manage alone, I'm no dope, I'll figure out an angle. Even if they stick me in some form of hell, I'll maneuver out of it, I'll slip right out like shit through a goose. That repentance thing might work, that voice said you can do it fast. Doesn't make sense to me, you mean someone like Essie lives a faithful life and someone else can do as they please and get away with it in one second of repentance. Sounds like too good a deal to me, sounds like I'm finished. I had my fun, what did I expect, one, two, three and I should smell like a rose?

I hear Essie's voice; she's speaking to me

"Now listen to me, I'm not fooling with you, this is it. Calm down now and stop rocking the boat. You're coming with us, we're going together. Don't tell me you're staying, 'cause you're not. I don't know the reason we're together but you heard Malakh, there's a reason for everything. And we weren't standing on that corner together except by the will of God. Now you had good parents, boy, maybe it's them helping to sneak you into the Kingdom, maybe it's that grandma of yours. Maybe it's something else we'll never understand. Okay. But I'm going to trust in the Lord, now more than ever. In your Bible and in mine it says to hope in Him, because we'll yet thank Him, even when we're down low, even when we're out. Now, you are heading out with us. We can't drag you but we're not leaving you here alone. I'm not fooling with you, I mean what I say."

I catch Mendel's eye, what does he think? He doesn't answer right away but then he smiles at me.

"I don't know what good it'll do you but I'll try to stick close to you. Who knows, maybe there is some mercy. I never saw it in my life but why give up now? My father didn't seem angry at me, maybe yours will forgive you, too. My father used to say a prayer—I remember it after all these years, he spoke it with conviction. 'Like a father has pity on his children, so may You have pity on us,' that was the prayer. Over and over he said it, he believed it. Maybe it will yet come true, maybe He'll yet appear."

"Clarissa, Brett," I ask, "any objections?" They both say no, they want me to take my chances with them. I appreciate the kindness, but what a bunch of *schnooks*. All

I can do is slow their progress, or worse. But what have I got to lose?

"All right," I say, "let's do it, I'm in."

"Malakh," shouts Brett, "we're ready! Can you hear us, we can't see you."

Our area lights up immediately and there he is, a big smile on his ethereal puss, the winner. Boy, I hate to give in, I'd like to wipe that grin off his face, I don't like to lose.

"Wonderful," Malakh strokes us, "you did the right thing. Now, in what order will you go? You of course realize that you must go one by one, single file. Each one of you will face the judgment alone. Who's first?"

They all look at me. I knew it, my goose is cooked. It's over.

Of all people, it's Essie who protests.

"No," she says, "we're going together. We're going to rely on the mercy of our Lord together. I didn't hear one thing in all our lives that deserves any one of us to be left out. If I could feel that way, won't the Lord whose mercies cover the world? We're together and that's it."

Malakh shakes his head.

"I've had it, I can handle all sorts of souls but not this combination of stubbornness and stupidity. You'll receive one more visit by an archangel, you'll be lucky if he grants you five minutes of his time. He's got North and South America on his back, he's a busy guy. Central America alone keeps up a steady barrage. And then there's Colombia, a big source of souls. Don't try his patience too much, he's got souls coming out of his ears."

Again we're in the dark and he's gone.

Before we can start talking, a fellow with a glowing crown floats in. He looks weary and distracted.

"Are you the group from the cult knife fight in the South Bronx?" he asks.

We explain that we're the Fifty-seventh and Park group.

"Oh darn," he complains, "I meant to do them first. Well, I'm here, so let's get down to business here. I'm the Archangel Gabriel. Never mind all that nonsense you may have heard about me, I don't blow any horns; I'm too old and it gives me a headache. I've been working my wings off since the Babylonian wars and I haven't had a week off since just before the first Crusade. So you'll have to understand that I view you as pests, just plain pests. Little uneventful lives. Who cares who you had sex with, big deal. You weren't nice to your mother, so shame on you. I'm dealing with heavy stuff and you're creating a bottleneck over minor issues. Hundreds of millions have been judged. They managed but not you? In ten years people down on earth will have difficulty remembering your names; in fifty years no one will. And all this loyalty to one another; you hardly know each other and back on earth you probably wouldn't have said a word to each other. Maybe Irv would have taken a shot at Clarissa but that would have been about it. The air is thinner up here, maybe it's affecting you. Get real. Just say the word, go through the process, most of you will be fine, one or two of you may have to shake, rattle, and roll for some time. So what, you can take it; you're not murderers, you're a bunch of ordinary mortals. Look, I've got to go now, there's some sniper shooting people in Mexico City. Think about it, don't be stubborn."

And he leaves before we can respond.

"Busy fellow," Clarissa says. "Now you see him, now you don't. And each one of these angels is the last one, the very last one. More last ones every few hours. There are stores like that in New York; they're always on final sale except they never do close. I wonder who'll be next."

We all look up. What is this? A woman is floating our way. Wow! They've got female angels here. And this one is a looker. Long red hair, big green eyes, and a shapely form. If it weren't for those sloppy, floppy wings of hers, I'd be tempted to chat her up a bit. She's a knockout and she's got a sweet smile.

"Are you an angel, too?" I inquire. "Because you're the first lady one we've seen."

"Yes, I can imagine," she replies in a tinkly sort of voice. "We've only recently been permitted to mingle with mixed-gender souls, can't be more than a thousand years at most that we've been emancipated up here. You don't mind, do you, our bodies are so diffuse and vague that it shouldn't matter that much. But if my hair is distracting you I can cover it up."

"Don't do that," I insist. "It cheers me up to see your pretty hair. What's your name?"

"Louella, just like your friend, that willing little British girl you took with you on your infamous trip to Stockholm. She was also sometimes a redhead although hers was dyed. Clairol, I believe."

"Gee, each of you angels know everything, every little secret of ours, it's amazing. No privacy whatsoever," I complain.

"Well, we're only trying to help. Only Malakh may poke his nose in again as far as I know, maybe at most one or two more. We've got work to do and I'm supposed to be very sensitive to your feelings. I hear you're quite a difficult group and that you're annoying everyone. So here's the story. If you don't proceed through the Court, only God alone can allow you over the Jordan, so to speak. Now He doesn't do that too frequently, and when He does it's only because the angels have totally failed. We are not kindly looked upon when that occurs. Gabriel himself has quite a temper and as for the mid-level angels they are very temperamental. And if you end up not getting into the Kingdom, you'll never be able to peek into the earthly world again. Now that's hellish, never to see your loved ones again. So it's my intent to give you a taste of what you'd be missing; only a taste, mind you. If you want lots of access to the earthly world, you have to cross over. But now we can pay a visit. No shrieking or yelling please, I find it too distracting. Who will go first?"

Nobody volunteers, been there, done that. I feel sorry for Louella, she's looking around, her eyes focus on me. Okay, what the hell.

"Me," I volunteer. Let's see what she comes up with.

The scene changes dramatically. My wife is sitting on a stone terrace overlooking the water. Looks like Westport or maybe Greenwich, beautiful homes, wonderful views. Jane looks older. Her hair is a pretty shade of gray, her manner open and happy as she greets two women and two men entering the room. She gets up, loud greetings are exchanged. Hey, that's her friend Helen and the other woman is that pesty loudmouth, can't remember her name, Gloria, I think. They both look a lot older, like old ladies.

"Is this in the future?" I ask.

"Yes," Louella replies, "up here past, present, and future are intermingled, hard to separate. All of it passes so quickly, the future seems to meld right into the past before you know it."

I don't recognize the two men, those are not those women's husbands, I know their husbands. And now a third man walks in, carrying a tray of drinks, must be his house. Holy cow, Jane is getting up at his request to bring in the hors d'oeuvres, what is she, his girlfriend? I recognize him; that's the alarm man who installed the system in our Bedford home, but he's older. Same dumb expression, I remember that stupid smile. I can't believe Jane would look twice at that putz; I think his name is Marvin. Yes, we always called that airhead Marv.

"Whose house is that?" I ask Louella.

"Why, it's Jane and Marv's country home. Jane will buy it about two years from now."

"What happened to my apartment and to my home in Bedford?"

"They kept the Manhattan apartment after they married but Marv wanted to be near his golf course so they moved."

"That asshole is living in my apartment? You mean he's there in her bed, in my bed, living together?"

"Why not?" answers Louella. "Jane wasn't the only woman you slept with in Jane's bed."

I'm speechless.

"I designed that bathroom in the apartment myself, every detail of it. The lapis lazuli floor, that lapis seat in the steam shower, even the toilet seat cover is color coordinated. You know how much that sink cost with those fancy faucets, what are they, Shirley Wagner, Sherle, something like that. That asshole is using my toilet, my sink, and she's letting him. What's the matter with her? She was supposed to be a lady, so refined, so damned old. What did she have to troll around and pick up this no one, this nothing, for? She'll belong in a nursing home soon, she'll get hers."

"Like your mother?" asks Louella sweetly.

"What about my car?" I change the subject. "Is good old Marv driving my car?"

"Don't think of it as your car," Louella reminds me. "Once you die, nothing like that remains with you, only your name and your memory. In those you don't drive."

Is she mocking me? Underneath that warm little smile, am I being ridiculed? She knows my thoughts, they all seem to, so I look her straight into her green, green eyes and wait.

She pauses, but then, "I suppose so," she responds. "Not very kind of me but I just couldn't resist. You evoke that kind of response; I suppose I feel some fellow sympathy with womankind when I think back over your life. You were a busy, busy boy. Now it's your wife's turn and at least she is married."

"I was married, too," I blurt out.

"One would never have known it," she replies, shrugging her shoulders.

"Will she be happy?" I ask. "Tell me, will she be happier with him than with me?"

"She'll be more admired, more respected, more adored by him."

"But will she be happier? Tell me, will she?"

Louella hesitates, even pouts a little.

"I hate to admit it but no, not really. She really loved you, you know, she couldn't help herself. The rest was just words; in the end, she loved you. She even forgave you, you know. Without her forgiveness, you might not be here in this group of souls now, you might have been headed in quite another direction."

My heart soars, then sinks. What did I do to her, how did I treat her?

"Enough," I say, "no more, please. Enough," and I let myself float slowly away.

Louella beams at the others.

"Who is next?" she cheerfully inquires. "Past, present, future, whatever you want, I can provide it. Or you can leave it up to me, like Irv did."

Brett makes a request. "I wonder about my funeral. I left enough money to cover the costs and I'm sure my sister came. But did anyone else? I'd like to see my funeral."

"Certainly," replies our angelic hostess, "with pleasure. Now don't be unhappy that there were not many people there—summer weekend, so many people were away. It was a graveside service. There's your sister; look how she's sobbing. You see, you were dearly loved. Oh, and look, another person is walking over."

We all now see a cemetery, an open grave with a coffin, Brett's I presume, placed by its side. An older man approaches, looks shyly at Sally, and then extends his hand.

When he learns that this is Brett's sister, he expresses his condolences. He's obviously self-conscious, looks warily about; I can well imagine why. The two stand side by side and wait.

Next to me, Clarissa gasps.

"So it *is* Tommy, it's really him. Look, if that was his problem, I forgive him. What could he do, he tried. I'm so glad it wasn't my fault. I suppose I can stop feeling guilty. It was long ago."

We all look down at the gravesite. Sally stirs.

"I don't suppose anyone else will be coming," she says. "I don't know why, he seemed to have so many friends. I'm so grateful you are here. Were you his good friend?"

She obviously doesn't know what Brett did for a living; otherwise what could she have expected? Tommy smiles at her, a pensive and sad smile, and acknowledges that he was a friend.

"Would you care to say a few words?" asks Sally.

Tommy looks about with some discomfort.

"I'm not really good at this," he answers. "Let me just say that I never had a closer friend, someone who really cared about me, someone who saw me at perhaps my very worst but always acted respectfully and kindly to me."

Brother, I think to myself, he must be kidding. These were financial transactions, with a tutu yet, what could he mean? He must be gilding the lily for the sister.

Brett is moved. "He's right, he really is. We were more than just client and, well, whatever you want to call me. If life had happened a little differently, we might have meant a lot more to each other. I can't believe he showed up at the grave. It took guts, it took character."

Clarissa interjects. "He always had that, he was always of impeccable character."

Sounds to me a little maudlin, a little hyper. The guy got his jollies and was sentimental about it, paid his last respects. Okay. I never remember feeling that way. For me, it was like a good meal; when it was over, you got up and walked away. To each his own.

But the visual lingers. We watch the crew bury the coffin. Sally and Tommy walk back to their cars and drive off. It is only then that a slender man walks out from under a nearby tree and stands in front of the fresh grave. He bends over and places a bouquet of peonies on the grave.

"My favorite—peonies," whispers Brett. "It's Freddy, he didn't forget. I forgive him for everything, the way he tried to erase me after those lousy pink drapes, the way he crawled back and became one of my best customers. Everything."

And we watch Freddy's shoulders shake as he weeps over the grave, while next to me Brett rejoices.

"He remembered, he won't forget me," repeats Brett as the visual fades.

"Anybody else?" asks Louella.

"Sure," replies Clarissa. "What I would really love to do is revisit Venice with Frank, or maybe my wedding day with Andy. Then there was Twinky's sweet sixteen. What do you think?"

"It's one to a customer, dear, you'll have to choose. I'm one of just three hundred angels in the Soul Service department and we are in enormous demand. Three hundred to cover all of the Americas and we don't just escort souls to their respective visuals, we're responsible for servicing all sorts of peculiar requests. I'm a jack-of-all-trades, so it's one request to a customer."

"Well," says Clarissa, "instead of a visual, could I ask a question? You probably will be clever enough to figure out the answer and with your female intuition you might just be my best hope. Louella, we five souls who died at Fifty-seventh and Park, were we there by sheer accident or was there a design in our being there? Five strangers and yet we've become so close. Was it part of a plan? Tell me, Louella. You're so obviously good at what you do, I trust you to tell me the truth."

"Compliments, compliments," chides Louella. "Do you think that I don't see through your compliments? Look, I can't answer your question directly but what I can do is give you a hint. Okay? Are you willing to give up your turn in exchange for a hint?" Clarissa nods affirmatively. "Paris," Louella says, "Paris is your hint. Now, while she mulls that over, anyone else ready?"

Mendel volunteers. "Years ago my wife and I planted a little garden in Jerusalem in memory of our parents; it's on the way from the town center to the Hadassah Hospital. Abe, that is Avery, helped us pay for it; he's a good boy, he always had a good heart. I wanted that my grandsons should see it, Abe was going to pay for me to take them soon. I'd like to see it once more myself now."

And we all see a small park in a modest-looking neighborhood, some benches, some swings, and a path winding through tall cypress trees. The mountain air is crystal clear and a few old ladies are sunning themselves on the lawn.

"I hope the boys see it," says Mendel. "I have no other souvenirs of my parents to give them, just this place. To me it always felt like a special place, a holy place. We would have stopped in Europe on the trip—there is a convention of survivors there—and then on to Jerusalem. But it was not to be."

"And now you, Essie, how may I help you?" asks Louella.

Essie stares right at her but she is silent. And yet, I can see from her expression that she is struggling to speak, as though something incredible has happened to her. Finally, she turns to Mendel.

"Where," she begins, "where in Europe were you going to stop and when?"

Mendel answers her. "Paris, the survivors meet in Paris, next month."

"Paris," Essie repeats, echoed by Clarissa.

"Paris!" shouts Brett. "Freddy invited me to join him on one of his all-expense-paid trips next month. I think it was on September twentieth—is that a Sunday?—I think so."

"I was booked into the Bristol, Andy and I, next month," Clarissa speaks up. "I was also leaving on that Sunday. What *is* this, what's going on? Essie, don't tell me you were going there, too. Were you?"

"I don't honestly know. Good Lord, have mercy, every year since Mrs. Perry died, my Patsy takes me on a trip but I never heard nothing about Paris. She took me to Mexico last year, God bless her, she never forgets me. I sure did a good job raising her with her kind heart. But I'm not sure where we were headed."

"Must have been Paris, couldn't be anywhere else, look how it fits," says Clarissa. "What about you, Irv? C'mon, tell me. Oh, my God, it's true, isn't it? C'mon, talk."

I can hardly speak, it's hard to respond. I bought those tickets just days ago for Jane's birthday. Paris and then down to Cannes, her big dream gift, twice before we had to cancel. What does it mean, what *can* it mean? I nod my head affirmatively.

"Essie, you have your turn left. Use it to ask her what this means, please, ask her," pleads Clarissa.

Louella suggests, "Stop right there, folks. I gave you a big hint, no more from me. Figure it out for yourselves. I'm an angel, not a psychic. So, Essie, do you have a request, any other request?"

Essie's wonderful smile appears, a wide one from ear to ear. "Yes, ma'am," she says, "please show me Patsy when she bought those tickets."

Louella tries to suppress her smile. "All righty," she says and we all see an attractive young woman inputting information into a computer.

"Please let me be closer, ma'am," says Essie. "Let me see real close. Thank you kindly."

And in unison, we all read PARIS.

"'Bye now," says Louella, as she fades away before our eyes. "I hope I was of service."

Part IV

Conclusion

We are all silent as we grapple with the issue. Obviously, we were all going to be in Paris if we had lived. But why should that tie us together? I didn't even want to go there, didn't want to spend my money there. And what would have been the chances that a poor, hardworking old lady like Essie would be traveling there? And Mendel, can you imagine him strolling down the Faubourg? What's going on?

"Let's think calmly about this," suggests Clarissa. "Let's not jump to any conclusions. Obviously, it was the trip to Paris or . . . maybe some accident or tragedy in Paris that would have affected us. But then why would it happen in New York instead? It doesn't make sense."

"Maybe not," says Brett. "Maybe none of us deserved to go; maybe we're being punished, we were not worthy."

"No way," I interject. "I would have preferred not to go. I have no liking for the French and who wants to be in shopping-central with my wife? It would have cost a fortune."

"Brilliant," answers Clarissa, her voice dripping with sarcasm. "So we died to save you from a big shopping bill. God, are you egocentric."

"Well, that sure wouldn't have bothered you; you and Andy must have been used to big bills."

"Stop," says Essie, "stop now. I don't know why this

happened but it shows who is in charge. The Lord, He made the decision, you can see there's a plan here. That's enough for me, I praise Him, Hallelujah. His eye is on the sparrow and you should thank Him. Thank you, Jesus."

Mendel comments. "For me this could be a blessing. My grandsons would have been with me, now they'll be safe at home."

"Yes, Lord," echoes Essie, "that's the way to look at it."

"My father always said that you give thanks over the bad as well as the good, I heard him say that a hundred times back home in Gyor."

"We have the same saying because the good Lord may send the bad to save us; sometimes He does that. He chastises us but He is strong to save."

"But think about it," I say. "If there was something bad waiting for us, maybe terrorists, who knows, then my wife would have been there, too, and your boys, Mendel."

"And my Patsy," adds Essie, "and your husband, Clarissa."

"And Freddy," whispers Brett. "I bet he'll delay his trip now."

"Maybe," says Essie. "This all might be the hand of the Lord. Hallelujah."

I think that would be comforting all right. But it's mighty convenient, maybe too convenient. I don't know, possibly we'll never know. But I'm happy Jane is safe; at least she won't be going anywhere so soon after my death, let her stay close to home.

"One thing I do know," Clarissa announces. "We're in this together, we're here for a reason. We should stick together; no one should separate us until we're finished with this difficult process. All for one and one for all, that's the way I feel."

And in almost perfect unison, we shout out our yeses, followed by Essie's repetition of "Yes, Lord."

Our little impromptu revival meeting is cut short by Malakh, who flies into our group looking aggravated.

"My God," he says, "don't tell me you're still here, still debating what to do next. I've got news for you, you folks can sit here from now to eternity without interrupting the Heavens. You'll just be in the way, like some old furniture. Despite your swollen egos, you don't matter that much. If you prefer to float about in this abysmal limbo, go right ahead. You want to miss what comes after judgment—the reunions with related souls, frolicking around in the next world after a bit of realignment and, in some cases, a bit of penance—well, it's okay with me. You like it here in the dark, fine, but if you change your mind don't count on me. I'll probably be busy elsewhere and you'll have to start over with another angel. And believe me, not every angel will be as patient as I am. Some of them will chew you up and spit you out if you don't follow orders. Me, I'm a softie, you don't appreciate how gentle I've been.

"I sent you the cherub; he usually charms the souls, but not you. And then Louella, she could snake-charm a snail out of its shell but she gave up. You may think that Gabriel is a little vague but he is high up on the totem pole here; one word from him and people fry or fly, nobody second-guesses him. And you blew him away. What am I going to do with you? Please, at least let me help you, Essie, and you, Mendel. You're shoo-ins and I want you to be happy. If I fail with you two, it'll be on my conscience. It will also be on my record. Why do you want to do this to yourselves and to me?"

Malakh actually seems to be emotional, his pained expression looks genuine.

He exclaims, "I'm so frustrated by you! Why can't you see that I have your best interests at heart?"

"I believe you, sir, I do," Essie comforts him. "But I also believe that there is a plan behind everything, the Lord has His reasons. We want to pass through into the Kingdom but I am sure that we should do it hand in hand. We died together and we want to walk on through together."

Brett adds, "That will give our death some meaning, imply some purpose. Otherwise, what was our death together for, just a matter of chance?"

Malakh answers sharply. "You're not supposed to know the why and wherefore, that's not your right as human beings. You're supposed to trust and to walk blindly on.

Your lives are made up of uncertainty and of untoward occurrences that must be borne. I know that Louella provided you with a hint; I wish she wouldn't do that but she's notoriously disobedient. Now you know much more than you should and what good has it done? You still distrust the system; you still trust each other more than you do the angels sent to guide you."

I can't take it anymore, I've got to answer him.

"We were given brains, weren't we? Aren't we supposed to use them? One minute I'm shopping for shirts and a minute later I'm history. I'm left with my brain and what you call my soul and a vague and fading body image. I'm supposed to become obedient when I've never been so, not since maybe I was a kid? I'm supposed to surrender my mind, my thoughts, and just go with the flow? That can't be God's will. If He created us He wants us to wrestle with Him, he wants us to think, to make our own judgments. If not, what are we like, chimps? Pavlov's dogs? All those struggles, all that suffering and misery, all those mistakes we made, and poof—all the lessons we learned are gone? Don't think, follow the angel, do what you're told. I don't believe it, I think you want to process us this way because it's easier for you. A day or two of your time and you're done, move those souls down the assembly line and give me the new batch. Isn't that right? Admit it, it's for your convenience, not God's."

Malakh doesn't even look at me as he replies. "There is only one more visitor you will have and he is not exactly an angel. I'm finished with you, I wash my hands of you. If any of you want to come with me, now's the time. Anyone?"

I look about. Nobody acquiesces. I wonder if I've misled them, if I've ruined their chances.

"Please," I urge them, "don't feel tied to me, go ahead if you want to. I've got issues that many of you don't have. Don't feel that you owe me anything, each of you choose for yourself."

Brett wavers. "Can I have any assurance from you that my judgment will be favorable? Can you give me some comfort here? Otherwise, I'm afraid to go alone."

Malakh says no, there can be no certainty.

"What do you think we should do?" asks Clarissa of Mendel.

"Me, I'm not ready to go to this judgment. We are told nothing of the judges, nothing of the rules. I want justice, a true judge, one that understands what my eyes have seen, what my heart has felt. I need to be given more time; the shock of death has not yet worn off. I need time."

Clarissa looks drawn, scared. "Essie, what should I do?" she asks.

"I don't rightly know for sure, but I don't feel afraid of waiting. Even if we just are left here in the dark, I know that I am not forsaken. It says that in the Bible, 'Though your

father and your mother may forsake you, the Lord will not.'
His eye is upon me and I am not afraid."

Malakh counters. "It also says to seek Him while He can
be found. When you're ready, He may not be. You're taking
a risk."

"You said we might have other visitors but not an angel,"
Clarissa reminds him. "What kind of visitor would that be,
Malakh?"

"You'll find out. Now, are any of you ready to come with
me? Yes or no."

Nobody speaks. Malakh shrugs and then disappears. We
are left in a dark silence; we feel safer together rather than
alone in facing whatever comes but it is a frightening
moment. Mendel is humming some tune quietly to himself.
Essie's eyes are closed, her face looks calm. Brett looks at
me and then quickly away. Only Clarissa seems in the mood
to chat.

"I know we did the right thing, I just feel it. I wouldn't
normally be so brave but I don't believe that there is a regular court, it doesn't make sense. Angels couldn't judge
us, they're different sorts of creatures; they couldn't possibly know our pain, our choices. And as long as we have
Essie and Mendel with us, I don't believe any harm can
come to us."

"You know, Clarissa," I say to her, "maybe this is the
judgment, maybe we've been through it and we are still

going through it now. Because I feel different from before, I don't even know if I'm the same person. I haven't had a mean or nasty thought in some time. I don't think I've even had a selfish one. Don't you feel different?"

"I don't know," she shrugs. "I'm just punchy, all this tension, all these decisions. I could use a nap, or what passes for a nap here. If you don't mind I'd like to just float near you for a while, close my eyes. You'll make sure I'm up if whoever is supposed to be coming turns up, won't you?"

"Sure," I say, and I watch as one by one the others close their eyes. Not me, I'm going to try to stay awake, to keep an eye on them. I feel responsible in some way for them. I was definitely part of the reason they stuck it out and I hope I didn't lead them down the garden path.

I am startled by a shrill sound, the sound of an approaching horn getting louder by the second. Everyone is now afraid and we all look at each other in shock. The noise is so overwhelming that it feels dangerous, threatening. And then, abruptly, it stops. The silence that follows is total and, in its own way, equally disconcerting.

Now light streaks through the vapors we float in, sharp bursts of light, soundless. And then the atmosphere trembles and shakes and we are pushed helplessly about by the ripples. It's only when I taste the salt of my tears that I realize that I must be crying.

Thank God, the ripples stop and we again float in absolute silence. What next?

A sonorous voice is heard, each word pronounced slowly and clearly and echoed again and again, seven times.

"With the permission of the Court on High, we will open proceedings," reverberating as in an echo chamber.

Believe me, I'm not about to argue, no protests here. If they want to judge us, they've got my permission. Enough is enough.

Out of the substance in which we float appears an awesome and monumental figure. It sports three sets of wings. One set covers what I guess is its head, one its feet, and with one set it flies. And this whole figure is aflame, burning brightly but not consumed. The only sound now is the sound of the flames which cover every part of the figure and of its wings, but no smoke rises from the fire.

Nothing is said, we float in absolute silence around the flaming figure. Are we in hell? Is there really such a place? Can't be, Essie and Mendel wouldn't be sent there and they are still with us. It's hard for me to think, I feel a growing sense of futility. Why did I fight back, what was I thinking? Who did I think I was? I avoid looking at the others, look what I got them into.

After some time, I hear Essie, her voice remarkably calm, no sound of fear at all. "You're a seraph, aren't you?" I hear her ask.

I open my eyes; she's smiling at the fiery image.

"A holy seraph, aren't you? My eyes have seen the glory of the seraph."

"Yes, right," says Mendel. "Of course. A seraph. Higher than an angel, holier. They exist, they must really exist. My God."

The seraph remains silent. But Essie is calm.

"Are you angry at us?" she asks. "Is God? I couldn't stand it if I made the Lord angry, please tell me He's not angry."

The seraph stirs. An astonishingly mellow voice emerges, a comforting sound.

"You are Essie Mae Rowder. We have been waiting for you. The Heavenly Court has been alerted, angels and cherubs await you, reunions and gladness are yours."

Essie is confused. "You're sure, sir, that you mean me? You got my name right. I'm the one from Bergen Street in Brooklyn. You mean me?"

"You have returned a spotless soul after eighty-eight years on earth. Of course, I mean you. We know how to celebrate a soul like yours up here. It's you, no one else."

"But the earrings, do you know about the diamond earrings? It only happened once. I'm so sorry." And Essie cries. "I never did it again."

"All your tears have been collected up here by the Court; they are precious up here, they sparkle more than diamonds, more than bushels of diamonds. All you have to do is ask for anything your soul desires and I am certain it will be granted. Anything and everything you want, you have but to ask."

"My grandson, James, he's named for my husband, I want him to change his ways, no drugs, but he should change through kindness, not through pain."

"Granted, not just James but your son and his whole family are covered. What else? Anything."

Essie looks around, shrugs her shoulders; she obviously can't think of anything else she's missing. But then she smiles.

"Oh, yes," she adds, "I want to go into the Kingdom with these souls here, I want to march in with them. We've been through the valley together. I want to climb with them, yes, Lord, that's what I ask."

The seraph replies. "They haven't been judged yet, please wait until they are judged. We have to see whether the Divine Mercy will overcome strict justice. But I believe it will since it is your request. So please be patient. I'm sure it will get done if that is your wish. Now, Mendel Perlow, you are next. You may address the Court."

Mendel seems relaxed. "I don't see a Court. Only you. Are you the judge?"

"There is a Court in session, although only I am visible to you. Everything is known here, you need not recite any facts to the Court. Simply speak to us, empty your heart. We know the suffering, the evil you have lived through. Speak."

"I have very little to say. Only why, why did God permit such a thing? Our little towns were filled with the study of the Bible, three times a day prayers rose to Heaven. People like my father lived from morning to night trusting in God, worrying they shouldn't sin, they shouldn't hurt someone's feelings. Poor brides were dowered, orphans were taken into homes, the sick were not neglected. We were not angels or seraphs but we tried hard to be *menschen*, to be decent people.

"And then the wild animals were let loose on us, worse than animals. People burned alive in our little synagogue, shot in the forests, spit upon, laughed at. Why? If I could have while I lived through it, I would have reached up into the Heavens and pulled this God of yours down into Auschwitz, into the slaughterhouse where He put us. And now my cousins with their children and grandchildren live in Jerusalem and the murderers are back, trying to kill us again. And not just that. The tsunamis, the famines, people killing each other in Africa, the AIDS, the terrorists. Where is this God? He sits in His Heaven and lets the world burn. Why, why?"

Wow, how does he dare, I'm afraid for him, he shouldn't have been so open. We all look at the seraph and we wait.

A terrible howl emerges, a wailing sound from the

monumental figure. The howl continues for some time. Then sobbing is heard and the sound of weeping. The seraph opens its top set of wings and we all see a terrible sight. Tears are flowing from the seraph's head, diminishing the flames for just a moment. The seraph's many eyes are wet with tears. We float there in awe until the sound stops and the flames increase again.

The seraph speaks. "It is not permissible for a human being to know why the good suffer and why the evil ones sometimes succeed in your world. Even we seraphs do not know; sometimes we cry out to the Judge, we scream out in pain. Such evil, such terror, and in each and every generation. Always new evil ones. Only the faces change but the evil remains. We were with you in the camps and on the trains, and we suffered with you in the pits and the killing fields. We suffer with all the innocent everywhere, we are aflame with pain and suffering, we burn with your sorrows. But none of us know the why, only the Judge. What you humans must do is try to live through the pain, and turn the suffering into some good. And if you cannot live through it, retain your trust; that is the test of every human being. I thank God every day that I am not a human. I don't know if I could pass such a test."

Mendel is not through. "But the children, the youngsters. Why them? Why?"

"I don't know, I've told you I don't know. A few times

I cried out, I approached the Throne of Mercy; look what they're doing, I cried, in so many places, decade after decade. All four of us seraphs who surround the Throne have cried out, have pleaded. The only reply is silence. Please Mendel, stop, stop now. Have mercy on me and stop now."

Mendel lapses into silence. The seraph seems to collect himself and turns to Clarissa with a question.

"You are next. Are you ready, have you a reasonable defense of what appears to be a life of considerable self-indulgence and of a married life riddled with deceit?"

Poor Clarissa. How can anyone answer such a pejorative question? But if anyone can worm out of it, she can.

She answers the question with one of her own. "Do you know what love is? I ask this with respect, I don't mean it as an insult. But do seraphs feel love? Once I know that, I'll be able to answer your question."

The seraph seems stumped. Some time passes as we wait for the answer.

"I don't know. I'm not sure," comes the reply. "I don't know how we could feel it in the way you humans do. We don't really have free will; we're messengers. Why do you need to know?"

"Because if you can't feel love then you may not under-stand my answer. Look, I was raised to expect love. I expected to marry and have a big family, a doting husband, a storybook romance. You know that all that eluded me. My first husband couldn't physically and Andy couldn't emotionally. With Andy I built a life, a wonderful life. A beautiful home, a splendid daughter, friends, money, the works. But always, always there was a gaping hole inside, an emptiness. I tried to work and I did a reasonably good job. My home was run impeccably and I helped Andy network for clients. I was basically a damned near perfect wife and he was a great husband. But is that it, that's all? Sometimes I think back to Venice, to Frank. What would he have been like for a lifetime?

"And as you all know, there was that incident with the pool boy, my one real adventure, my one pathetic little secret. Look what happened from that so-called sin, look, my wonderful daughter, Andy's comfort and support. Better that anything that I ever succeeded in when I stuck to the rules. And just to add to the confusion, I'm condemned for shopping! Okay, the few instances of shoplifting were outrageous, unpardonable; I just couldn't face another argument with Andy about the bills. But the shopping itself, should I be condemned for that? So in my lifetime I bought a dozen alligator bags I didn't need. Maybe three or four alligators were killed to make me happy; I can live with that. What else did I do? Make myself happy or at least distract myself with some foolishness. In the great march of humanity, that counts as a sin?

"Give me a break. I think I've been entitled to whatever pleasure I've derived from my shopping and, believe me, I'm far from alone. There are lots of equally desperate and determined shoppers out there. Take a stroll through Saks or Bergdorf's, look at those compulsive women, those glazed looks, those passionate expressions. Ever visit a Gucci store during their semiannual sales? Thank God for women like me, whole retail empires depend on us. Look, seraph, I know I'm being judged, I know I appear to you to be a foolish little woman but I'm through trembling. I've had it. If I've been a bad person, I didn't know it, and it's too late now to change anyway. So it's up to you now, I'm at your disposal."

The seraph makes no comment. He simply turns toward Brett.

"And you, Brett, you were an able and educated man. Why did you choose to live as you did? Where was your ambition? Man was designed to work and to create by the sweat of his brow."

Brett seems annoyed; his expression changes from his usual poker face to something steely. He floats just a little closer to the seraph and speaks with feeling.

"I am really, really tired of having to defend myself, to explain myself over and over. I don't mean to be insulting but, hell, I didn't exactly ask for my life. Nobody consulted with me before they put a full-fledged, softhearted, warm, and cuddly girl into the body I was given. Nobody asked permission before giving me what one of my clients called the most beautiful set of thighs in the Greater Metropolitan Area—and let me assure you that good thighs are harder to find than a good conscience or a good heart. They are a lot rarer. I would have been just as happy with a bald head, big ears, a flabby middle, and the heart and soul of a man.

"And what talents other than the ones I used to make my living did I have? My career as a decorator was short and disastrous. I suppose I could have driven a taxi or served soup and sandwiches. On the other hand, making over $150,000 a year tax free seemed a tad more alluring. And who said my brow didn't sweat? A lot more than just my brow sweated. You obviously haven't seen too many, if any, of my working sessions. You think it's easy, jumping around, pretending ecstasy while trying not to be crushed by some man who needs a shower? If I had been a plumber or a waiter I'd be admissible to the Kingdom but because of what I was I have no place there? I'm not even bringing up my mother and how I treated her or the way I still loved my father when he stopped loving me. No, no. I want justice. I want to know why this trick was played on me, giving me a certain nature and then condemning me for it. If you find out, why don't you just let me know?"

Damn. It's my turn, Brett looks like he's finished. Maybe I can use his *shtick*, I can blame God for my fooling around, why did He make me so sensual? Or he could have created me ugly and poor and then I wouldn't have been successful at it. Ugly would have been all right, but ugly and poor makes you a loser. Money to a woman is the ultimate aphrodisiac. I could blame it on being granted wealth. I've got to think of something fast, the seraph is turning my way.

"Irv, after the last two soliloquies, I can hardly wait for your little speech. Don't think that I don't know what you are thinking but I would like you to articulate it, nonetheless. The Court requires it because it forces you to think through your life cold-bloodedly. So proceed if you are ready."

But I'm not. Give me a break here, I'm plotting out how to reply even though they know my every thought. And what can I say, I was as unfaithful a husband as I could be, I was about as self-centered as was humanly possible, and I very rarely made a charitable donation that didn't redound to my benefit. As to my business career, about all I can say is that I wasn't arrested, but I don't think I had better dwell on that area. And as to my paternal performance, well, who knows? I've been paying for Bobby's psychiatrist for eight years and I'm sure I bear some blame for his problems. And Jane, she suffered, she knew all along. I ended up abusing her. But I'm tired, tired of all this self-analysis, why did I do this, why did I do that? I'm beginning not to care. Okay, I wasn't perfect, but I worked hard, I created businesses that employed a couple of hundred people. That's bad? I wasn't a monster. In fact, I was generally nice to people who depended on me. I certainly never bragged in front of anyone less successful than I was, that much of a *shmuck* I wasn't. All right, so I put my name up on the hospital wall or at that fancy museum, so arrest me, I'm guilty. The Irving and Jane Caldman Hall of Contemporary Art, for this I should fry. Who did I kill, what do they want from me?

I look up at the seraph. I've tried almost everything else, maybe I should try the simple truth.

"Seraph, I don't really want to answer your question, I wouldn't be proud of the answer. I can tell you're no fan of mine. Why don't you just do with me whatever you want, because I can't take anymore. You think it's easy to realize that after sixty-four years I didn't ring too many bells, that if I'm lucky maybe four or five people will really miss me? That if it rains really hard at my funeral, half the people won't bother to come? I did try to achieve some things; I don't know what happened. Look, I'd like to see my parents one last time before you do whatever you have to do with me. Then I'll be as ready as I'll ever be."

Essie pipes up. "You are something, boy, you are really something. First you argue and wrestle with those angels and do whatever else you are big enough to do and now you're just plain giving up. Like an old mule, just can't kick anymore, huh? But I'm still right here, still kicking, and this holy seraph here made me a promise. And seraphs are no liars, believe you me, none of them are liars. And I have a living God who sure doesn't lie. He is no liar and that you know well. They promised me that you are all going into the Kingdom with me. You said that, seraph, you said that the Divine Mercy is trying to conquer strict justice and sure as I'm floating here I believe it will. I believe it always does. He's our Father and in the end He can't help but forgive His own."

The seraph answers. "I'll ask the Judge. Remember, I'm only a messenger. Let me check for you, Essie."

"That's not any old judge you're talking about, that's the Father of us all, that's the man who makes the sun come out and the wind blow and the sea roar. He made us and He knows how weak we are and how short our time is. He'll have mercy on us. This lady here, Clarissa, she had a hard life. Maybe she decorated herself, maybe she loved her shoes, her fancy shoes, but with no peace inside her she was a suffering soul. Don't anybody make light of her pain. She never knew how to be satisfied, she never learned how. She was empty inside, that's not her fault. If you're not loved up and down and sideways, no one can feel right. She never had the comfort of love."

Essie looks at Brett. "And that poor boy there, all those men pawing at him. He just got lost, that's all. And then he died before he could turn things around again. He never had his chance. You think he would take such a path if he had the choice? He was young, he fell into an easy trap. You've never been that, seraph—young and human. It's mighty hard to stay clean before the Lord. Don't be too tough with him."

Essie's eyes fill with tears. "Mendel, he's a man of sorrows, he offered up plenty of suffering. That should be as good as prayer in the eyes of God. Only He can judge him."

Now her eyes rest on me.

"And look at Irv. Look how his spirit is broken, and I know that the good Lord doesn't turn away a spirit that is crushed. No way."

She floats up toward the seraph.

"I know what you're thinking, seraph, you think I don't know? You're wondering who is Essie to speak so plain to you? I know I'm just flesh and blood but I've grown to love these souls. That's what we're supposed to do—love, right? And it's not easy in our world. The devil is plenty busy, sometimes it's hard just to keep going. And I know that I didn't do the best job with my own boys, I was so busy raising Patsy and I could have done better with my grandkids, too. But in the end, I punished them and I said harsh things but I loved my kids. So I forgave them out of love and mercy. Now we're standing before the Father of us all and expecting a miracle. I'm standing firm and expecting signs and wonders. Because He is mighty to save, mighty to forgive. He sees it all, He knows it all, He made it all. There's not even one movement of the wind that isn't by His will, not one grain of sand that He doesn't have in the palm of His hand. I'm trusting in

Him, I always have, and I'm not stopping now. I love Him. I know He won't fail us now. So please make way for us, we're heading up, and we're going together. We've agreed and we're expecting a miracle. Hallelujah."

Essie's face is aglow with conviction that energizes the rest of us. Even Mendel's expression has brightened and the rest of us huddle close to them both. Maybe I really have a chance here; I knew if I stuck with them I might make it. At least I've got a shot.

Slowly, languidly, we begin to float upward while the seraph blazes above us. Wondrous sprays of light now shoot through our space and we hear a triumphant blast of a ram's horn, one long piercing note. Then we all pause in awed response as the atmosphere trembles mightily. We look at one another for support and for strength. The seraph, too, pauses in mid-ascent.

And suddenly everything stops, freezes. The trembling stops and a heavy, thick silence descends upon us, a silence you can feel, you can almost taste.

A still, small voice becomes audible, almost a whisper.

"Seraph," the voice instructs, "hear My voice. My children have won the argument, they have prevailed. I am proud of them, they have bested Me."

We are surrounded by a singular sound, the sweetest, warmest laughter I can recall. And the last words I hear as I begin to ascend are, "What children I have, they have bested Me."

ACKNOWLEDGMENTS

If anything in the literary world is more difficult than having a first novel published, it must surely be the publication of a second one. The first might prove to have been a bit of luck. The second one indicates an author's good fortune in prodding a publisher into a repeat performance. I therefore would like to express my gratitude to Will Balliett of Carroll & Graf Publishers and to my literary agents, Kim Witherspoon and David Forrer of InkWell Management, for their confidence in me and for their enthusiasm on the path to publication of this book.

But this novel might never have been written were it not for the persistent efforts by Carolyn Starman Hessel, executive director of the Jewish Book Council, to convince this sixty-seven-year-old businessman that more than one novel lay within his power. To quote her, "If not now, when?"

My children, Michael and Sarah Freund, Rebecca and Eddie Sugar, and John Freund, edited and reviewed the manuscript; and I am grateful to Tina Ponzo and to the late Sonia Sorg for their typing and editing skills. But, of course, everything ultimately depended on the verdict of my wife, Dr. Matta Freund, who read the final version and did not order me to cease and desist. For that, I am truly grateful.